Weeds Beneath the Open Meadows

Anna Casamento Arrigo

PAGE PUBLISHING, INC.
New York, NY

First originally published by Page Publishing 2013

ISBN 978-1-62838-024-8 (pbk)
ISBN 978-1-62838-025-5 (digital)

Printed in the United States of America

For all children who dare to dream
My dad, who–among other things–taught me the value
of an education
My husband for his unconditional love and support
My children who are in each and every breath I take
And for the sister I wish I knew

Preface

*"The keenest sorrow is to recognize ourselves
at the sole cause of all our adversities."
- Sophocles*

It was a season when young girls and boys were told who they could marry; where white line was hung out in the fresh air after a union; men owned land or cultivated it for the benefit of others; children ran to the ruins of a convent of long ago; dogs yelped on the cobblestone roads or sought meager scraps of this or that from the village's only butcher; ownership of a goat, like my nonna's, placed you on a higher rung of the proverbial ladder; gypsies caravaned up the hills and along the ocean view, up the solitary path that lead to this small village in Sicily, called Sorrentini; babies were dropped from the occasional plane that flew in sun-filled skies; Hershey kisses were signs of wealth, adventure, fortune; death was never made to look pretty, prepared; hints of the wayward, the connected-the reputed Mafia soldier, the American sent comparis and commaris whispering behind closed doors; a season when everything planned happened; everything happened that was planned; and a season when the unplanned changed everything, something, and nothing simultaneously. A season when the only proof of life, before this time of bullet scars, foreign vinyl albums from which a sound cascades over a child's ears filling her with delight, pleasure, and rhythm. Where all else fades away, the guns high up, supposedly beyond a child's reach, in the two-door armoire; where legends and fairytales lighten the hearts of three children huddled close in anticipation of the night's barb. A lesson. A moral. All is good in this land not so far away. A season when a girl watches, with a keen eye, the comings and goings of her aging father and suspects, though never questions, or asks why. Why does papa travel so often to America, the distant land where the streets are paved with gold, and dreams are reality?

A season of escapades, charades, tirades, untruths, and everything in between. When a journey, like all journeys, means goodbye. Not farewell, so long, see you soon. Just goodbye. Like death only not. We surmise that death is the end. Or not. Either way, a journey.

X   X   X   X

Chapter 1
Journey

"Everyone is born a king, and most people die in exile."
- Oscar Wilde

Although I read somewhere that we are not our thoughts, I also know, realize, that our thoughts define us, if not in part, then, in entirety. Our experiences, after all, become our thoughts. And, it is in these thoughts that I find a puzzle. Paradigms. State the truth and nothing but the truth. Right! What I may find to be the truth often, however, belies a rationale and purpose. It is elusive, intangible, and as such, more complex than merely stating it, makes it so. Whose truth might that be? Exactly how important to know it or to even care, the truth being a subjective thing after all.

State the facts and just the facts. Again I am puzzled. Because, again, facts are subjective as well, an image in a mirror; sometimes reversed to fit our needs, yet most likely and most especially over time they are found on their own journey from one mouth to another's.

The only mode my thoughts run in, though, is rewind. Never fast-forward and certainly never stopped. Thus the truth is my thoughts and, the facts are my experience, subjective, and still mine.

Chapter 2
Facts

"We do not do what we want and yet we are responsible for what we are-that is a fact."
- Oscar Wilde

On November 9, 1968, my father died. He was seventy-seven and I was twelve. While there may be some discrepancy over the date of his birth (whether he was born on April 6, or April 9, 1891), it is a fact that he was seventy-seven. I was twelve. Of all my memories, those I consider most powerful, important, worthy of remembering and good, his laugh, which to the best of my recollection, didn't happen often, was full. It was one of those laughs that comes from deep within where, I imagine, the diaphragm gets pushed, full force, against the lungs like a power driven engine just let loose upon it, and it fills the air and lingers in the walls, the furniture, reverberates to the mice and roaches lying in wait behind those laughter covered walls. That, the laughter, not the mice or roaches, was the best laughter I've ever heard.

But it's November 8th, the night before the journey, and I am at the end of cleaning the remnants of a busy Friday night at my aunt and uncle's pizzeria. Although they're not really my aunt and uncle, the relationship is complicated for a twelve year old; Sicilian culture deems that those who are older are to be respected and addressed as aunt or uncle, or at the very least,signora or signore. I ask permission to visit my father who is in Christ Hospital in Jersey City, recovering, though not very well; clinging to life to be perfectly clear, from an operation he had just a few days ago.

They cut into his stomach or that part of your body that holds the stomach, which doctors determined was the cause of his bloody vomit and phlegm producing cough. He is recovering. It wasn't his first trip there, however, just last week, he had been taken there to be medicated from what, the doctors and nurses surmised to be bronchitis or pneumonia. This visit, after having been released after one week of intravenous medication, was repeated one day after this release. He woke to a coughing fit that sent his body into convulsions and bloody sputum. Yet, here he is once again hooked up, this time to oxygen and tubes hissing his recovery.

Even as a twelve year old, I know he can't possibly be recovering. My father, whose laughter sometimes filled the air, whose phlegm found its way to the garbage bag next to the dinner table, who walked with a cane he really didn't need; who had nine other legitimate children with his first wife, and then three more, including me, with his present forty year old wife. In reality, though, it was never discussed; he probably could have fathered a few more – and most definitely did – in both Sicily, and Jamestown, New York.

Yes, now he is on yet another journey; not like the ones he made to Sicily when I was younger and not like the ones he made to Jamestown, New York, where his other children from his previous marriage lived; and it wasn't the journey to visit his other two from his mistress either. I, on two occasions had accompanied him on this journey: one time with my half-sister, MaryAnn, and the other just with my dad.

Jamestown, NY, where I, the one who would one day go to college, bragged by father, would spend time with his hated daughter-in-law and her two children, Ronnie, who was in his late teens and Marlene, who was just about my age. Marlene, who made it known that my place was that of guest, nothing more, and who made it known that she tolerated me because she had to for her father's sake; her mother hated me and my father, she had said. Ronnie, on the other hand, doted on me and made me feel welcome and comfortable and made me my first ever lettuce and tomato sandwich on white bread with mayonnaise. I couldn't believe the burst of flavors that filled me and wished I could have more. My father strictly admonished me, "never ask for anything more than is given," he said.

Journeys on trains to Jamestown where I remember MaryAnn taking off her shoes and tapping her baby powdered feet on the seat in front of us, sending me into muffled tears of amusement. I loved her so.

I loved the trip to her apartment on 87th Street in North Bergen, where she prepared my breakfast of eggs, bacon, and toast, each Saturday and Sunday morning. Where she often rested on her chaise afterward, drink in hand while I ventured out into the playground in the complex. Where children of all ages, with their clicks and foreign ways ridiculed me. Their English almost understandable, I was a quick learner (dad would have it no other way), when they had their fill of my obvious foreign ways and dress, began speaking an altogether even more foreign language, Pig Latin. Thus, I would often make my way back up to my sister's apartment by way of one of two elevators. The creaking, the dinging, and I making our solitary ascent. Once there, my sister would make my lunch and take her place back on her chaise until dinner and an hour of nightly news; a welcome break in the silence. And on rare occasions when MaryAnn was in need of this or that, or simply needed to get a message to her husband, who often was not home, but rather at the bar on 82nd street, I would be sent to relay these correspondences.

"Grunt, hum, alright. Tell her I'll take care of it," he husband slurred, and off I sauntered back to the apartment on 87th Street. Sometimes, on very rare occasions, I was fortunate enough to hang out with my nineteen year old niece, who had found her way home from this escapade or another. Her room was off limits, like a sacred temple, menacingly guarded by unseen specters. I relished the times she would turn her hi-fi or radio on and show me some dance moves. "Satisfaction," by Rolling Stones was by far my favorite.

But unlike those journeys to MaryAnn's house, or to Jamestown, this journey unlike the one where mom had accompanied dad to Messina, Sicily; this journey, with his then thirty five year old wife and three children,was over the turbulent water of the Atlantic to America by way of Canada. This time, my dad was journeying alone and left my mom, me, my brothers, but also MaryAnn far behind. I wondered if Maryann would ever come to visit us as she had each and every week when dad was home; I wondered how she would spend her time and her few glasses of whiskey with, now that dad was journeying. Would she still come with arms full of clothing she no longer wanted and give them to my mother? My mom, who would thank her somewhat gratefully, begrudgingly, stored them away, never to be seen again. MaryAnn who made me breakfast, lunch, and dinner and who would often sit on her chaise, glass in hand while her husband sat with his cronies taking bets and drinking, drinking until he'd finished his business or run out of money for booze, I suppose. Who would come home in the late hours, like a specter, making his way, stumbling down the hallway past MaryAnn, past me, without a word, past his only daughter's room, to his bedroom, shutting the door behind him. Yes, I wondered if things would ever be the same as they were before dad was off on his journey?

Begging the night clerk at the front desk at Christ Hospital, he first looked at me quizzically, with those piercing brown eyes that revealed nothing and everything to the twelve year old wanting to visit her papa. He agreed to allow me a few minutes. Not truly understanding what a few minutes in the greater scheme of things meant, I thanked him excitedly while his firm voice echoed the vast hallways, "Don't let me come up and get you."

Making my way to the elevator, I'm uneasy, questioning my motives. Did I really want to see him? After all, I'd only been there this morning and perhaps, somewhere in his mind and mine, he'd rather journey alone. I made my way to the elevator just as I had earlier that morning and just like I had on my previous visit two weeks earlier. Two weeks earlier, he had been taken to the hospital after his return from a journey, a quick stay in Jamestown, New York. He had had occasion to visit his other, older kids, quite often, actually, in Jamestown. This last time, however, was different and as the elevator ascends to the third floor, again, I question my need that eluded me still.

My mind wanders as the elevator ascends and I think of his return, his many returns. Two weeks ago was one of those returns, yet, somehow, he had changed. He coughed up phlegm continuously and catching his breath, he mumbled to my mother as his nineteen year-old grandson bared his weight and guided him to the bed he and my mom shared. We were, my brothers and I, scooted away to the kitchen to find something to eat or do; we understood we needed to go somewhere that would not allow us within earshot. Hastily, Little Joe, his grandson, who I had met only briefly on one of my two visits to Jamestown, as I recall, drove a speedster and dated often. I remember, he asked his father, my half-brother, Big Joe, (who had years earlier changed his last name to Casel, a change that angered dad at the mere thought of it), for some cash for a big date.

"You better take the big truck then." His father responded. I found this rather funny, although I was just eleven, understanding the humor of it. Big Joe owned a car dealership in Warren, Pennsylvania, with a house on its lot, as well as a store selling everything from fruit to furniture. Mentioning to my dad on several occasions, the need to expand the facility on that side of the street where yet another house stood, but as I had heard Big Joe mention, he didn't want to go through the expense of it all. Yes, Big Joe, who owned not just this dealership and store, also owned the house across from it where he kept his latest mistress, who was sometimes accompanied by his and her child

One of Big Joe's many mistresses, who had visited my house on Franklin Street in Jersey, stayed for several days, and tended to my needs, combing my hair and talking girl talk, and whose departure left me crushed and crying. She left me with a promise to return and a promise to send me a doll by carrier (neither of which was kept), just miles away from his home, a home he shared with his wife and their six children. A home where his children were admonished for trying to leave the dinner table before everyone else had finished their dinner.

A home that, for all intents and purposes, appeared the ideal home talked about and imagined by the villagers I had not so long ago left behind; a home that had one more bed for me when I visited on one of those two times and sometimes two if Joanne, Big Joe's eldest daughter, was off to college. A home that dad visited and where dad and Big Joe would spend hours whispering behind closed den doors. A home which dad visited but never stayed. A home that had the room, but one in which dad never stayed. I never questioned where he went or where he slept. Even at ten and then at eleven years old I knew enough not to question the comings and goings of dad with his boxer hands and full laughter.

Perhaps, he's at his cousin's house, or one of his other children's houses. After all, three of them lived in Jamestown, not to mention his daughter, Josephine and her husband and two grown children; a ranch style house with a massive backyard, where their children had set up a net still leaving enough room for ten more nets if they had chosen. Later, on one of my two visits, they tried to show me how to hit a badminton birdie to no avail.

I liked visiting then and felt a pang of regret for having to leave it behind when dad decided that we could not stay because there would be no work for my mom in Jamestown, NY. And I wondered, even then, if that was the only reason for having to leave.

Still, we left the furnished apartment dad had rented on a weekly basis during the hot summer month of July; we had just weeks earlier, the upstairs apartment just above the fruit store, of Aunt Katie and Uncle Joe. It was West New York; our first stop. It was here that Aunt Katie happily greeted us and made every effort to accommodate her returning brother and his family. We remained there for just two weeks or so before hurriedly leaving in a hustle and frenzied rush knowing that things had been said that related to money—money that dad had previously lent to his sister and her husband and now asked for its return. It was not meant to be.

Off to Jamestown, where dad would leave for hours on end and return sometimes in the late afternoon, sometimes in the late evening. Jamestown, New York, birthplace of the great Lucille Ball. A city surrounded by the suburbs that nestled split level, colonial, cape cod homes all with neatly manicured lawns and bright flowers.

Visiting his elder children, perhaps, helping Big Joe in his store, but leaving us, his young wife who spoke no English and her bored children to while away the hours staring out the window waiting for something that never came.

It was also in Jamestown, on a very hot and humid mid-July afternoon, that mom, who had enough of her children's banter and pleadings for something to drink besides water, gave me 35 cents to buy a bottle of soda down at the corner store. Off I went, money in hand, happy to do so. Dad had brought one home days earlier, though I couldn't remember seeing the container itself; dad poured each of us a glass and the container was gone just like that.

"Soda," I asked. It was a word dad had said and easy enough for me to remember. I would buy soda and return to our ill and outdated furnished apartment in the middle of the city.

The woman behind the counter spoke a language I did not understand but I simply responded with the only word I knew as she patiently waited for me the perplexed, embarrassed, look upon my face certainly giving me away. Again, she spoke.

"Soda," I said.

Coming from behind her place behind the counter, she motioned me with her outstretched hand to follow her. I did. Up one aisle of boxes and cans, the likes of which I had never seen. Until finally she stretched up and reached for a bottle. Never having seen a bottle before, (such things did not exist in Sicily in 1963) I shook my head and shrugged my shoulders. Her undiminished patience, the gentleness of her nature, and a smile that reveals the soul of a compassionate being, just like that; she continued taking bottle after bottle down off their assigned spots and returning them after each shake of my head.

"Soda," I repeated after each and every presentation.

I expected her patience to grow thin. It didn't. She walked me down another aisle and presented me with a box which I took, perhaps because I anticipated her patience would eventually give and partly because, at this point, I feared my sweaty, drenched dress and red face growing impatient and perhaps worried about the delay of her wayward daughter. I took the box neatly placed in its brown bag, paid and quickly raced out the door and back down to our apartment. I climbed the stairs with great anticipation of having our thirsts quenched and our fatigue from the great heat relieved.

My mom grabbed the bag I presented her, peered into it and was somewhat befuddled.

"The woman said this was soda," lying for the woman, even if she had said that, I certainly couldn't, didn't understand it.

Mom opened the box, grabbed a pitcher and gradually added the white powder into it. She poured a generous glass for each of us. We drank expecting the fizzy concoction to fill our sense with sugary, bubbly refreshment. Our noses crinkled simultaneously, it seemed. And rather than spit it out, we swallowed. We stared one to the other. "Maybe it needs sugar," I offered.

Without question, mom grabbed hold of the sugar bowl on the table and spooned in several scoops into the pitcher. We tasted again.

Again we crinkled, winced, and mom added more sugar. It was no use. Suddenly, mom's face contorted as if she had just been hit with an invisible mace.

"Ma chi si stupita, chesta e bocarbonato!" she bellowed. "What are you, stupid? This is baking soda!" She poured out the remaining mixture and placed the now almost empty box into the cupboard.

"It says soda on the box." That one word was, in my mind, universal. It sounds as it is spelled. It's soda even in Sicily; that's how they would write it. I was convinced of this. Neither my mother nor my brothers, whose anticipation had been readily crushed, believed me. Back to the window; welcome to America!

I remember mom recounting the happening to my dad upon his return, his full bellied laugh filling the rooms. The next afternoon, dad brought in several bags, all filled with bottles of Seven-Up. Dad called it soda but, for the life of me, I don't recall those words jumping out at me. But I do remember there were no more trips to the store.

But it's years since then, and on this rare and only visit, Little Joe, with his tousled blond hair and his father's piercing blue eyes, bounded down the stairs only to be followed, shortly thereafter, by a ring of the doorbell. One of my older brothers, who visited our house often with his variety of mistresses, and had been known to be quite a hard ass, and had his bouts with the law, bolted through the door to my father's room and summoned my mother to his side. By now my father was wheezing and coughing and everything else in between words. The door was closed and an ominous feeling engulfed me along with the mice and roaches that lay in wait behind what used to be laughter covered walls.

"If anyone comes, anyone at all," my older half- brother warned, "you are all to say that pop has been here and has not left Jersey for weeks! Do you understand?"

Not really, I thought. But at twelve, I knew enough not to challenge or ask questions of my elders. Just as quickly as he came, my older half-brother, left. He left, leaving his heaving, wheezing, coughing, father behind in his bed; leaving three anxious children, my older brother, my younger brother, and me to wonder why such instructions were given. It wasn't so much the questions that frightened me as the answers might have been. And yet my mother repeated the warning, not missing a

16

step as if she had the answers and, for certainty, she would not share. "You say nothing." She said. End of story and she closed the bedroom door to nurse her husband from whatever was holding him hostage and preparing him for his journey. The remainder of the night was spent tending to my dad. My mother, on occasion, summoned me to get another washcloth or a new paper bag for his sputum. All night she kept vigil, as I lay awake and would rise to catch a glimpse behind closed curtains, carefully sliding fingers behind the lacey material, all to catch a glimpse of the comings and goings of no one in the middle of this restless, frightful night; waiting for the ringing of the bell that would allow entrance to those wanting to visit; or a pounding on the door if the downstairs inner door had not been pulled closed behind those exiting. My mind was pacing back and forth in thoughts of policemen coming and forcefully, uncaringly, in total disregard of his present failing health, taking my dad away.

"Anna? Another wash cloth! Then go to bed!" These were the last words I'd heard my mother say as she once again closed the door behind her and my wheezing, coughing, spewing dad.

I liked my nineteen year old nephew well enough; his blond hair, his fun-loving energy. Still, I wondered why he couldn't stay and visit;why my older half-brother couldn't stay and visit either. There were so many questions. Papa was home and had been home for the last few weeks. I recited these words as the elevator slowly crept up. Interminable, slow elevators. It seems things move more slowly when you're in a hurry like anticipating a holiday or a birthday gift that awaits your eager fingers. Then, once it arrives, it's often met with, "Now what?"

Chapter 3
Innocence Past

" This miserable state is borne by the wretched souls of those
who lived without disgrace and without praise."
- Dante Alighieri

Ding! First floor. Again, I feel that uncertainty, the dread of finding death. Alone; just me and the sound of my own thoughts ascending this ill-lit encasement they call an elevator, making my way to visit my journeying father. Ding! Floor two. I'm riveted back in time, not too long ago, within these confining, slow-ascending walls. I discover, in my own twelve year old mind, a great distraction in things past; things that have kept me up at night; things that are hidden, secretive. I am seven, eight, nine, ten, eleven, and twelve all over again.

Once upon a time not so long ago, in a not so far away land, lived a little girl who loved playing in the mountains and meadows near home. Hours upon hours, her friends and she, played Ring Around the Rosie, freeze tag, and collected flowers in the meadows to make laurels for their heads. While the occasional gypsy tracked their way up the mountain trails, the somewhat curious and free-spirited young girl, dressed in the skirt that Nonna had hand embroidered pretty flowers along the suspenders and down along the hemline, would throw caution to the wind and taunt and tease those traveling caravans, and throw rocks along the way. Don't know why for sure, except, it seemed to me, people often went running for cover whenever they heard those jingling bells up the path.

In my mind, I was showing the courage that Casamento's were known to have, or I was simply an idiot. The last time I tried that stunt, though, I was nearly abducted, at least I've been told so; I too would go into hiding usually in a lush bush along the path; they just fascinated me, those wondering gypsies and with their jingling bells and tambourines excited me. The rock throwing was Anna being a Casamento.

"What are we do to with you?" chided Nonna, who often watched over me while my mother and older brother traveled to a place that even a curious child was not privy to know; and when mom didn't travel with my older brother, she took journeys with my American father who sometimes visited; stayed for a while overseeing the men working our olive orchards or grape villas or spending time in the village's only café; he could often be found there playing cards with others, who referred to him as the American, and, while appearing honored by his mere presence, were also known to fear him.

Perhaps, it was this same juxtaposed emotion; fear and honor that convinced this twenty-four year old woman, my mother, to be swept off her feet, set up house and become pregnant with his child. The first born while he was on one of his journeys back to America, Sal. My father, he was never daddy, though dad was okay, just never call him pop, lest you wanted a swift backhanded slap to your face. I never, inquisitive as I was about all things, understood why; and in reflecting back perhaps the sound was too close and served as a reminder of a gun, which he often carried or slept with during the night. And it wasn't just that one gun, he had several, everyone knew. No questions asked; his father had been murdered when dad was only twelve years old,and his entire family was whisked away during the course of that same night. Off to America, somewhere around the year 1908.

Dad rarely wore shirts that revealed his collarbone, his upper arms, or his legs. He, I suppose, didn't need to show his battle/bullet wounds to remind anyone of what or who he was and how and when he got them. Literally, the villagers parted ways when he approached and more fantastic still, I suppose, is the fact that our home was constantly filled with this villager or that in dire straits, and even more fantastic, he never seemed to turn anyone away. Money exchanged hands and the occasional treat, fruit, chicken, or grain was left in its place.

Between 1908 and May 8, 1963, dad made several journeys to that not so far away place where his father, Nicholas, had been gunned down. Even I, at the age of five, knew by then that his first journey was to settle the score as per my paternal grandmother, Maryann, a strong steadfast woman who wielded an iron fist and whose temper matched it; who left this village with three children in tow and one on the way. He never traveled steerage according to a document I found years ago, nor did he or his nine children from his first wife, whose name coincidently enough, was also named Anna, suffer during the Great Depression. Though dad often called me MaryAnna, and yes, I responded.

It was sometime around 1950 that dad made yet another journey, swept, or intimated or threatened (I'm not sure I want to know), a young girl of twenty-two off her feet. She was the daughter of his friend, my Nonno, who had spent years with dad working the Eerie Lackawanna Railroads and where my dad had invited him back to his home back in Sicily on his next journey. Dad, at this point,was fifty-nine when he took my nonno's invite quite seriously.

He denied his first born shortly after he returned and unknowingly, I am told, that he had left this twenty-four year old girl pregnant; no wonder he was so suspicious. Anyway, he accused his friend, my nonno of being the father and couldn't stand the young toddler especially since the only one who could soothe and bounce off his knee was my nonno and not dad. Off to America for another short visit.

Upon his return, his wife became pregnant yet again, and this time he was certain it was his. Yes, his that is, until the child turned out to be a girl.

"That's impossible!" said my father. "A fortune teller told me I would never father another girl." My mom often recounted this story to me and the details were always the same; dad said not to feed you and would hold me back so that I couldn't come and take care of you. He even tried tying my hands behind my back she had told me.

So here I am. He fathered a third child and had remained for the duration of that pregnancy. A year later, he returns again to America and the arrival of the occasional care packages begins. I never realized how much I cared for those days; buying candy is a rarity and candy kisses from America made an impact and commanded this mother of three, who continued supervising the men in the fields in his absence, respect. But months turned into a year, then two, and a young woman of thirty-three gets restless. She has an affair with a doctor in the city by the sea and he even offered her marriage, and to adopt the American's other three children; this was something that never came to fruition.

The American returned with an engagement ring and a promise to take every one of us back to America with the understanding that the Doctor's child be put in an orphanage. And so it was; we journey on The Queen Frederica to America. My mom still an Italian citizen and we, since they got married just before boarding, were on dad's American passport.

The streets of America were paved with gold and money, the villagers had said, but they were mistaken. Gold was not found in the streets as we had been led to believe. In fact, my mother, who had never sewn a day in her life, learned quickly since that was the only job that would accept an immigrant with no skills. Mom was a quick learner though and actually managed to get a second job (dad had known people) sewing linings to fur collars that would be attached to coats. Seven years old and, I too, am learning how to sew linings. Mom and I sitting away hours upon hours, sewing piece work (the more productivity, the greater the reward). Mom, however, also worked the factory, as seamstress during the early morning hours till five or six. She quickly ate the meal dad had prepared, and set off to sew those endless linings on fox, mink, or some other poor creature, that would adorn the exclusive coats of those who didn't know their collars were sewn by a seven year old and her newly arrived young immigrant wife. Who would, each and every payday, present him with her earnings. He in turn would hand back a few dollars and pocket the rest.

Dad looked for a house. But the unavailability of jobs for mom and the proximity to my dad's first family was more than my mom could bear. Thinking back to our very first day in Jamestown, I recall a gathering of most of the family members at Uncle Tony's house (my father's cousin), where even dad's first wife, Anna, was invited. A gentle woman, as she seemed to me, with a kind face that solicited dagger stares and suspicious glances from my mother. She gave a Hershey Bar to my brothers and me. I quickly and excitedly ran to my mom to show her my treasure.

"Throw it away, now," she admonished. "It's poisoned!" I looked at my Hershey bar and then back to this gentle woman sitting at a distance. I stared at that treasured Hershey bar, gathered my brothers, headed to the garbage can nearby and reluctantly, grudgingly, sorrowfully, threw them all away.

Mom had later recounted that dad had said he did not keep contact with his ex-wife and hinted even at her death. She was alive and well and, without any words exchanged kept a very wide and comfortable distance from my mother who sat staring at her hands, her feet, the grass, the house, while not once, even for a fleeting instant land her eyes on my dad's first wife. The hate permeated the air and but for the interest in my younger brother's mishap, he had gotten his pinky finger caught in the folding chair, and cut it badly. Anna came over offering help, rushing, ordering her children to get this and that to stave the bleeding while, Pippo, screeched, whimpered and huddled closely to mom. He was quickly taken up in my dad's arms and he and Uncle Tony, who owned a car, drove to what they called a hospital. Fear instantly crept in on me; a feeling of dread that somehow I would never see my brother again. Huddled close to my mom, we sat, my brother, Sal and I, waiting for what might happen next. Not a word was spoken as we waited. Finally, after what seemed like hours, my brother, Pippo, came running back to where we had been sitting brandishing a bandaged finger and propped himself up on mom's lap, his finger had now become the symbol for courage and attention. Both were short lived, however, as each reassigned themselves to their prior conversations leaving Pippo, Sal, and me to huddle even closer to my mom and her chair away from the others. The accident was followed by that now familiar distance and quiet once again.

Thus, we moved to Jersey City, an apartment at first, and, a house months later. And so my life's a sad song. I had to relinquish my earrings so that people wouldn't readily know I was an immigrant as well as my nonna's beautifully embroidered clothes.

When we finally moved into our apartment house with its minimal yard space and noisy neighbors, I realized things were going from bad to worse. Those gypsies cursed me with the ability to see trauma before it happens and it does so in my dreams and nightmares frequently.

The people whose apartment dad bought, had three children, one who had just turned seventeen and wanted me to play a game that had some rules; parents must never find out because they would not go through with the sale, they would call me a liar; it would be my fault; besides who would believe such a wayward immigrant girl of seven?

I was to keep my eyes closed and follow directions carefully; and say absolutely nothing. So this is America. A land of opportunists and deviants. Yes, he had me pull down my panties, guided me to a bed, and rubbed along my vagina.

"You like this, don't you?" the son asked me."Bet you do it with your brother too?" My eyes closed, his voice grates against my neck. Bewildered, his young five year old sister and my five year old brother, having been commanded out into that space called a yard, frighten me still further.

"Can I look now?" I said through clenched teeth.

"No," he said sternly. "And shut up, or I'll tell everyone about you."

I wished at that very moment I was back in our four room rental with rope binding my feet to the side and my hands bound to the chair's armrest. I had stolen a nickel or a dime or even a quarter that would buy me those pretty teenage girls on a front cover, begging to be released and dressed up in those beautiful clothes that had to be punched out as well.

I just never learned that when dad would take his afternoon naps, after all he was in his seventies, and the occasional job at the Stanley

Movie Theater near Journal Square; the same theater that dad would clean, gathering the discarded and uneaten candy for his three children waiting for the night's bounty; and yes, we ate those pawed and discarded candy with gratefulness. Dad had thought enough to bring them home for his young Sicilian children who long ago opened fresh packages of Hershey kisses.

And so, tired after hours of cleaning and walking the two some odd miles home, he counted each and every coin in his pocket before placing his pants over the solitary chair in his room. But I think to myself that, one day, when I went to the A & P with my dad,he casually took a pack of cigarettes from the cashier's overhead shelf and never paid,but my taking a coin is not okay?

So here I was again with my old familiar friend whose second hand purchase made me happy and sad even when I wasn't tied to it, I'd sit in it and imagine those now faded flowers rich and lush. My brothers having been sent out to amuse themselves, tried to sneak peeks in the large front window. It was there that, if one leaned far enough over the rickety wooden rail, one could catch, full view of that faded throne, the one that held me tied down, the one that dad had used to hold my small frame as he beat me with his belt-my legs, my arms and whatever else the leather or buckle would land upon. It was there that my brothers, from that peek through that they would whisper words of comfort until my mom came home.

"It's alright, Anna." They would say."Mom will be home soon."
Soon. Soon enough as I sat and imagined my life back in the meadows with a laurel wreath upon my head, dancing to the rhythm of the wind and the gentle wisp of weeds and fauna. Where the flowers were never faded and one could imagine a simpler, happy life without so many adverse conditions.

But today, I am bound and my free spirit is collecting faded flowers, I am running in that not so far village and collecting flowers for my laurel, I am a princess who has been captured and awaiting my liberator; mom's home, unties me, reprimands my now drunk father, and pretends with my hand in hers, to look for that coin that must have dropped out when dad took his pants off.

"Let's look under the bed, Anna, that's probably where it rolled. What was it, Sam?"My mom asked. I never understood why she never

24

called him Salvatore, his given name, or at the very least, Sal. "A nickel you said? Oh, look, there it is. Anna, reach in and grab it and bring it to your father." Dad looks straight at me, then to my mom, then back at me, and takes a slug of his whiskey.

The same whiskey that followed us to Franklin Street when we bought our home, where innocence is not so innocent, and dad cries when he doesn't get his whiskey as expected. It had been a terrible brutal rainy day and mom, as she had explained to her anticipating husband, did not have an umbrella and the extra blocks to the liquor store were more than she could bear on this icy rain day. "Sorry, Sam. I'll get it tomorrow."

He cried. Yes, dad cried. Dad did not have his whiskey as expected. I had never seen my father cry. Mom scurried about the house, sending us out of the kitchen and consoled her grieving husband as best she could.

"I promise," I heard her murmur repeatedly.

Mom, Carmela, age 24. Dad, Salvatore, age 61.

Chapter 4
House

"By a small sample, we may judge of the whole piece."
- Miguel de Cervantes

"You better give me that," said my five year old brother. "Or I'm telling what we did," he threatened.

"Go ahead," I said. "I'm not giving you the Tammy doll Maryann gave me last Christmas. You've already chopped her feet and cut her hair."

"At least you got something. And I've been as good as you. That's not fair. I'm telling. Mom!" He bellowed. "Guess what? Anna had me playing house with her while you were at work and dad was out."
It was true; I'd played house with my brother and now he had told. I imagined the chair again and was ready. Those belt marks had not healed since the last time.

Mom grabbed the rope immersed in salted water, removed my skirt, held me up by my hair and started the beating. Blood trickling, tears flowing, and the brother eating his dinner with his grubby little paws shoving noodles into his mouth.

It's funny how things have changed. Today, when a child is sent to school with even a tiny scratch in New Jersey, red flags go up all over the place, and DYFS is called in. Not then. The nurse looks at my legs, scowls, takes my temperature, which is well over one hundred degrees, and sends me home.

My dad picks up his wayward daughter from a friends' house (no one will come to our house: one; they're terrified of my father; two; I have linings to sew). And so it goes. He's holding me alongside him all the way home,throwing hits at me in any way he can, when a patrol car stops.

"Hey,"screamed the officers. "You stop hitting that child."

"Keep on moving," my father responded."This is my daughter, and if you don't keep moving, you're next."

And so I'm hit for the next three blocks until, finally, at the front stoops, he flings me through the door, down the hallway, into the house and on the chair next to the box of collars awaiting their lining.

And so for years, I went to school, came home and did my homework, then, if there were linings to sew, I would start just to give mom a bit of a break. The harder I worked, it seemed to me, the less I got beat and so it went, day in day out. And on those rare occasions when the collars that needed lining did not get dropped off, I went out to play with a girl named Wanda Ortiz.

We played School. More often than not, I was the teacher and she the student. When she finally moved, I was in sixth grade and had been in a tracked class (the powers that be thought me gifted). Gifted indeed.

If nothing else, though, dad had said to his family that I would go to college. Funny, how that one, otherwise positive word, can so negatively impact one; you see, in Sicily, when one referred to colegio, it meant orphanage. Hearing that word, I immediately froze and resigned myself to believing that as a wayward girl, I had finally pushed my dad to his limits. And my fate, like the half-sister I never knew, would be the same; put into an orphanage.

"Dad," I said knowing there was no going back now. After all, what did I have to lose? I was going to an orphanage anyway. "Why are you sending me away to an orphanage?"

My Uncle Tony, to whom he had been bragging about his intelligent, wayward girl, and he, began to laugh, again a full laugh that left me even more puzzled.

"Dad?" I waited for an answer.

"Anna, in America, colegio means college." He told me.

"College? What is that?"

"That's where you go when you finish your studies in the lower classes."

"Oh." Not truly understanding the whole idea still, for the moment I was more than grateful not to be going to an orphanage. My half-sister, the one fathered by the doctor, the one I don't remember except for what my dad told me when he and mom were in one of their horrible fights, went to an orphanage and was never seen again. I was just glad I wasn't going there too.

On days, when I felt lonely and isolated, since no one ever came to our house, I so wished I had a sister. A sister with whom I could share secrets; a sister who wouldn't judge my waywardness; a sister whose secrets wouldn't have to be her own; a sister who would understand and see how my mood would change when the adults were occupied with work, or travel, or drink; a sister who would be there to share the memory of a real wild flower covered meadow. It would never be that. No. That sister was left in an orphanage.

"See that statue there, Anna?" My mom would point out each and every time that she and I had those all too few moments together in the land no so far away. "Behind there is the orphanage."

No further words or explanations were needed. I understood. But, honestly, all I could do, all I could remember, was the statue; a beautiful bronze statue of an angel watching, perhaps guarding, the angels within. I was such an optimist, I suppose. Everything, I believed had a beauty if you looked, believed deeply enough.

But deep within the roots of my mind, I wondered what this half-sister looked like now? Who she resembled; was her hair as dark as mine; were her eyes chestnut brown like mine; did she ever collect flowers in the meadows; who was this sister I wished I'd had?

And just as important, to me, as those questions may have been, I wondered, even cringed, at the thought of what it felt like for my mom to give up her daughter to a place no one ever visited, and whose inhabitants the villagers were often heard loudly and affirmatively calling bastard children of whores.

My mom was not a whore; lonely, confused, overwhelmed, gossiped about behind closed doors, whose care package had not come for months on end, and whose love affair had left her making the ultimate sacrifice. She chose to save, to enrich the lives of three, and so I wished I had a sister.

Chapter 5
Ding! Floor Two

"The truth is forced upon us, very quickly by a foe."
- Aristophanes

"If any one comes and asks questions, just make sure you tell them pop (that's what my older half-brother called him. And if dad heard me call him that, it would have been followed with a quick slap from his boxer hands. Just like that) has been here in Jersey City and has never left. Do you understand? He's never left Jersey City?"

Understand is such a silly word yet it holds so much uncertainty and even now, as I wait for this unending ride up to visit my recovering father, I wonder if he would have understood or used his great boxer hands to punish the baker as well.

Dad loved fresh bread, usually on the weekends; thankfully it was only once in a while. We didn't have a term for men like him back then; but dad wanted his bread, and I knew enough not to say no to dad. I always admired, my father's ability to size people up, but for some reason, he never realized that the Anna who went to the baker's was not the Anna who returned, and he never understood why I wouldn't eat the bakery bread; understand. I dreaded going to the bakery on Palisade Avenue from which the scent of freshly baked good wafted to the very core of each and every cranny of each and every house along Palisade Avenue and beyond down to our house on Franklin Street. From a distance, the aroma of the bakery intoxicated my senses. But the closer I got to the doors, garage doors really, the greater the dread. I'd pray that the woman or owner would be there today and not the baker who often took over when the owner was out on deliveries. It usually didn't work out that way. Freshly baked bread lined the case and table adjoining the hinged counter with access to the higher shelves that housed more freshly baked bread.

The first time the baker said I had to be lifted onto his shoulders and get the bread with my own hands, I didn't question it. He was, after all, older than I. So, he lifted my eight year old frame onto his shoulder and waited for me to reach for the bread.

"Just grab the one under the others, but don't drop any in the process," he sneered as his hands found their way up my skirt and to my panties. After rubbing his flour caked paws in my private area, he slowly, tightly slid me down, with the fresh baked bread now in my hands, his body.

It was the same when I went to the pizzeria to work for my Uncle and Aunt. If I timed it correctly I could guarantee that my aunt would be there and not my uncle or, at the very least, both would be together. Unfortunately, nothing comes with a true guarantee, I've discovered. I thought my fifty something year old uncle truly cared about me; so when he asked me to sit on his lap in the bathroom where he was supposedly putting his shoes on, I expected a fatherly hug and genuine concern for this child who had no friends to speak of and all she seemed to do was work. That wasn't the case. He talked about how pretty I was, and suddenly that same sense of hate I had going to the baker's came over me. It must be me. I lived with the shame of being a girl unworthy of love, compassion, and understanding. I wanted the free-spirit who picked flowers in the meadows and made laurels waiting for the prince to come.

Ding! The door opens to a faintly lit hallway. Hesitantly, though I'm not quite sure why since it was my decision, my choice to visit. I made my way down the corridor to his room. Maybe I shouldn't have had that fight, I think as I approach his room, with my 'cousin' the one whose parents own the pizzeria. And suddenly, I wonder does she sit on her father's lap and get told how pretty she is? After all, she often likens herself to Sophia Loren. I'm thinking, girl, you just got big boobs and that's the only similarity I see. And yet a part of me envies her, not her money or her supposed likeness to Sophia, but the ease with which she can announce to the world that she's a virgin. Here I am, twelve and have seen and experienced unmentionable things that lead me to think I am not. What does she know? What has she done? And a small voice in my own head is saying, What girl in their right mind goes around announcing to the crowded pizzeria floor that she's a virgin and intends to remain that way till she's married? So much for marrying, I mutter to no one in particular.

The pizzeria and Sophia are far behind me. Still, I'm thinking, thinking. I'm thinking as I get closer and closer to dad's bed. Wires, tubes and hissing sound of oxygen as it fills his nostrils. It echoes and somehow, though it defies explanation, soothes me. I'm not sure why, but they do. His eyes open. He's staring up to the ceiling. Fixed. I look up to that imaginary spot, where his eyes are fixed, wanting, wishing to see what he sees. Nothing. I watch his eyes, his face, and just listen to the hissing that replaces the laughter that filled the walls and the mice and roaches behind them. Oh, don't be fooled. I'm sure there are mice and roaches here as well. Why else would there be a need for an exterminator's truck to visit the hospital on a monthly basis just like our house on Franklin Street.

His eyes are fixed. I say nothing. I watch. I listen. A vacuous space filled by hissing and an empty stare to an object, something only dad can see. Dad and his secrets. Dad who has never left Jersey City! Still, I stand there watching. Time.

The clerk said, "Only a few minutes." Has it been a few minutes? Has it been few enough? I say nothing but angle myself over my dad and look straight into his eyes. The same eyes that had had several operations. His lower lashes kept finding their way into his eyes with excess skin that had to be cut and re-cut. Twice a year, the doctors would admit him to St. Mary's in Hoboken for the day so there was no need to visit. The eyes that had surgery twice a year were fixed upon that spot; that imaginary spot like the one I would take myself to when I was tied to the faded flower chair.

Dad: with your hands bound to the side rails, are you taking yourself to that imaginary spot? Those beautiful hazel eyes that had surgery twice a year; those hazel eyes that required a save to help the healing process; those eyes that only eye dropped that magic potion after his

31

surgery; now, as I watch,his eyes are fixed on his imaginary spot. I wonder, "Dad, did you trust me after all?"

I stood ever so still watching, listening and still said nothing. Hiss. Hiss,whir, shir, and a gurgling now filled the walls. I left him that night with his hazel eyes that said everything and revealed nothing. I left him with the echoing hiss of the machine that helped him breathe. I said nothing as I made my way to the "Ding!"

Past the night clerk with a simple nod and "thank you." I left my dad to his journey.

Chapter 6
November Came Slowly Soon

"Though it be honest, it is never good to bring bad news."
- William Shakespeare

The slow moving November air captured my prayer, "God, if you're listening, please take my dad if he's going to suffer like this."

I don't know why I said it, where it came from, or how it reached my lips on that cold November night. God, I believe, unlike other times, times when I would pray for the callous hands of molesters and abusers that ravaged my young body and stole my innocence, had listened. This prayer, he heard.

The tubes and machines would stop their ear piercing whirring, echoing buzzes that filtered the hospital walls and reached the mice and roaches that hid there in wait for silence, would stop; and a young mother with her three children would readjust and move on in this world, this America, without the seventy-seven year old patriarch, who drank often and physically tortured my older brother and me. No longer would I feel the brutal force of his boxer hands as he hit this wayward girl, leaving welts upon my face and legs.

No longer would knives go flying midair, aimed at my older brother, who had irritated him in one way or another. Never would he wake my old brother in the middle of a sound sleep and greet him with punches and slaps waking him to screams that filtered through the walls of our new apartment, our roach and mice infested house. My heart broke for him then, for as many fights and arguments that siblings often shared, I loved him deeply. I reflected back, rather than face the truth of what Sal was going through at my father's hands during the still of the night, I reflected back to the times I had been tied down and Sal and my younger brother would peer through the bay window while standing on the front porch and make those funny faces and whisper their words of comfort. Yes, I submerged my aching heart in those memories of soft whispers and imaginary princes coming to rescue the damsel in distress. Who would rescue Sal?

"Sam," my mom would urge, "that's enough. Let him sleep." And so he did, leaving his now fully awakened and bruised son to quiver and whimper, as I tried desperately to block those all too familiar sounds of anguish and pain from my mind. It, the escape into my own mind, never worked. I lay quietly in my bed until my eyes shut and sleep nestled me in its womb.

Yet, it was also those boxer hands that nurtured me when I was ill. Nurtured me and tried desperately to annihilate the growth, the one under my left breast, which the doctors had told him needed to be watched and saved with a scalding hot towel. He would boil water, ring it out with those same boxer hands, which had now been tied to his bed rails, ironically reminding me of my own bondage, and lay it upon that bothersome growth. It never went away. No matter how many or how often the scalding cloths or his boxer hands that found gentleness and caring as he placed them on my breast.

Never would he rummage the drawers for the most recent documentation that showed that our shots were up to date; he never could find them. Thus, once again, for what seemed a periodic event and journey, once again, to the Medical Center on Montgomery Street in Jersey City; Medical Center where a gathering of citizens waiting their turn for this medical necessity or that, would stare at everything, everyone back and forth. An awkwardness that we all shared, our eyes meeting if only for an instant, a passing glimpse and a sense of wonderment as to why we might be here waiting. He was a curiosity, this seventy something year old man, and three young children.

Funny, how we all come to our own truths as we sit and wait. For a young child, the truth is not often as complicated as those of adults. Yet, as I had once before experienced, while dad and I had made our way to Central Avenue and the fruit and vegetable market, they must all be thinking this way, a gentle grandfather with his grandchildren in tow waiting, like them, for the nurse to call them into through the clinic doors.

"Little girl," the fruit and vegetable vendor had shouted as he refilled his bins of this and that. Tell your grandfather not to touch all the tomatoes. Tell him to take what he wants and leave the rest alone."

"He's not my grandfather, he's my father!" I retorted with my small, firm Casamento voice. My father who was now on his journey.

Chapter 7
Tiny Steps Backwards

"It is easier to resist at the beginning than at the end."
- Leonardo Da Vinci

Ring! Ring!

Startled and awake, I picked up the black receiver that sat on the black dial phone with its faded hue that rested upon the second-hand mahogany table which had been bought when we set up house. Though it was not really just a table,it was actually a table adjoined to a chair, though I don't ever remember anyone sitting in it to talk on the phone. Not even dad, who was in the hospital recovering from surgery; the oxygen I heard hissing and echoing down the ill-lit corridor. My dad, who carried a cane he really didn't need. My dad who made his own wine in the damp, musty, dirt laden basement of our four family, two storefront, home on Franklin Street in Jersey City. Wine I delivered to his friend who would hand me two dollars and sometimes, though not often, would hand me a nickel or dime for my journey. Since my dad, didn't believe in soda or milk, he often would give my older brother, Sal, and me, some of his homemade wine for lunch.

Mom at work, it was one of dad's responsibilities to feed us lunch. That, and making sure my homework was done upon arriving home before I set down to sew those linings. Wine was, after all, not just a passion to occupy dad's idle time, but a staple in our home.

So it was wine. Wine that dad had spent days upon days crushing in the vice over and over again and storing the juices in his enormous wooden barrels, that quenched us. Unfortunately, it was also at one of these lunches that my brother, Sal, had a bit more than a nine year old should have, if any at all, and went to school drunk. Sal was sent to the nurse, where she assessed his demeanor, took his temperature and sent him home with what she thought was virus accompanied by fever.

My dad hand-picked those beautifully scented grapes, for their perfection. My dad who, in the spring and summer months, would prepare the tiny plot of yard into rows of neat piles of earth in preparation for planting tomatoes, eggplant, basil, sweet peppers, and onions. My dad could often be found sitting, hose in hand, allowing the water to gently trickle on to the budding seedlings freshly planted and carefully tended to under his watchful eye. Dad, who sat sputum coughed up even under the morning sun and heaved up with little difficulty and, with head to one side, let it fall to the ground beside that faded, rusted, aluminum chair. Dad, who exuded delight and pride as the crops, his crops, came to full bloom and ready for his boxer hands to gather them all for his wife and her three children.

And on those days, when he wasn't on his rusty chair, he could be found sitting with the shoemaker in a rickety old chair on the ground floor of our house. It was there that he could be found, more often than not, retelling tales of times gone by; and it was there, upon entering, that all conversation stopped. What secrets they had shared, I could only guess; a fact that I sometimes, the wayward child, would sneak peeks without their spying me; there the past unfolded. There, my dad and his shoemaker friend, who smoked crooked cigars that smelled of old, smelled of death, smelled of something long gone; dead; the smell that filled your nostrils long after you had left the store; a mixture of new glue, old glue, and crooked, twisted dead cigars and old men and secrets.

But it is November 9th, and the phone on the second-hand mahogany table rang just twice. The same phone that, at whim, I would pick up, when no one was watching, just to see, hear a forbidden conversation by unknown faces; it was a party line. It wasn't until I was caught, by either one of my parents or those unknown voices, that I let the receiver fall back onto the faded holder. Often, the conversations were nothing more than the boring tales of this one's dinner plans or the latest gossip, neither of which really interested me in the least. Still, it was something to do; something my greater imagination could draw upon. And on those days when no one was watching, no one was on the party line, my brother and I would dial a random number from the phone book and prank yet another disguised voice, a gruff voice, a tired voice, or one with no feeling in it all.

No, this call was none of those. No, I would not be sitting to answer the wakening, startling ring that came in the early hours on Friday, November 9, 1968.

"Salvatore's taking his last breaths. You need to come quickly." This was all I heard from the unseen face.

Groggy, half-drunk from an unsettled sleep, I became lost in those words. It couldn't have been that party line communication I'd heard before. We were anonymous. Those times had been planned, wrong and rude, eavesdropping on conversations of those faceless voices on the phone that rested by our entrance between two bedrooms; my mom and dad's and the one that was used by my brothers and me alternately. And on the occasions, when one or two of us wasn't in that room, we would sleep in the, what I call, the 'passageway room' that led to the bathroom, the living and, at the back of the house, the kitchen. Such were the layouts of our corridor like apartment on Franklin Street.

No, I was not eavesdropping this early morning, very early morning, before the rise of a November sun. It was not someone else's conversation I'd heard. They were mine. They were my mom's. They were my brother's.

"Salvatore's taking his last breaths. You need to come quickly." The voice had said.

And come quickly we did. Dressing. Running fingers through our hair. Slipping shoes on and slipping out the door.

Quickly is such an odd word when embarking on a journey. A journey that makes a few city blocks seem like the crossing of the endless sea.

When will we ever get there? Last breaths?

I'm thinking how many breaths exactly might that be. Is there someone actually counting?

Salvatore's taking his last breaths and we're coming quickly.

And as the chill of that early morning November morning snipped at our faces like the jagged claws of a wayward claw on some shore of the distant past, we walked each step taking us closer and farther simultaneously.

Down Palisade Avenue. Down the isolated, noiseless, faintly lit streets toward Christ Hospital. Past the pizzeria, 212 Palisade Avenue, where Sophia Loren had picked a fight the night before; the fight that had sent me to visit my recovering dad with his eyes fixed and the echoing hiss of oxygen within a one-bed room of a dimly lit hospital corridor. The clerk, the one who said I could visit for just a few minutes. The one who reminded me, not in words but in a soft nighttime pillow welcome look that reminded me I was only 12. A 12 year old visiting her recovering dad after nine when all visitors had already found their way home.

A clerk, much like the usher, five years earlier, guided my brothers and me to the front of the ship's movie theater long after the movie had started. Three young children; my older brother, just 9, my younger 5, and me. On a journey, at seven, a journey to America from Messina, Sicily. The port city miles from our small village of Sorrentini. Sorrentini, the small village that as nestled beneath Mt. Etna. The village where all of my best memories would remain; where Nonna had hand sewn my green and then my blue light corduroy skirts with their suspenders and borders of meadow flowers; where my friends still could be found playing in the meadows and fields or hunting snails after a heavy rain, all this in my mind's eye remained the same; my village.

But this is Messina, Sicily where we are bound for America on the Greek ship, Frederika, sailing third class in April with an approximate date of arrival to the land of gold sometime in early May 1963. Messina and its busy streets and buildings taller than any I had seen save for Patti, another larger village near my village, which overlooked the sea more directly than Sorrentini had. We board with the luggage long before carried by wheeled contraptions; and at seven the idea of others taking possession isn't easily understood even after assurances from one savvy passenger, my dad.

My dad, who'd traveled across the Atlantic Ocean on several occasions, and now, what would be, unbeknownst to him or his young family, his last voyage. In the time leading up to his final year, he had made meticulous plans to re-visit Sicily. His dream was to discover water, a valuable commodity in those parts, and provide a greater existence for his family. I'd watched him open packs of cigarettes, take a few out and then re-wrap the lesser contents of those packages and shove them down into one of the many 'water' pipes he planned to take with him for his water line.

"They charge for transported cigarettes." I heard him say to more than one person on more than one occasion. Thus it continued; buy cigarettes, un-pack, re-wrap, shove, and start all over again. There were many pipes which he kept locked in a make-shift closet (a remnant of a door that had at one time led out to a wooden balcony from the kitchen). The outer opening had long ago been covered with plaster board and haphazardly painted. It provided a great storage place for these pipes with their treasures. Along with these however, were other treasures. It was dad's passion and, perhaps his frugal nature as well, to dry his own homemade sausage. While he meticulously chopped the large butcher fresh pork into cubes; some for fresh, ready to eat raw or wrapped in block paper and thrown (Sicilian style) into the open flame of our 1930s stove; some dried and hung in that treasured place of the kitchen. It made perfect sense, especially since the rats had gotten to the one, the previous year, in the basement. It wouldn't happen here; he was right. Even the rats knew enough not to mess with his treasured place. And it wasn't unlike dad, who after trapping one of those creatures and putting an end to it, to lift it by its tail and hold it trophy like for all of us to see.

That was then. Here we are aboard the great ship taking us all to the land where all that is possible may very well come to fruition. The Frederica where dad walks with ease and, to none of our surprise, was comfortably home. Passengers, perhaps on the same journey, heading for the same destination, made way, parted for this, albeit elderly gentleman, passenger with his family in tow.

Settled in for our voyage, it came as a great surprise that dad had no qualms whatsoever allowing his young children free reign of all the ship had to offer. Leading the way, with my younger brother's hand in mine (since it was my responsibility to safeguard him for as long as I could remember), and my older brother alongside, we meandered up and down stairs and down and through this corridor and that at will.

We this all while my mother, rested, vomited, complained, turned green, moaned, vomited, and rested some more in the cabin. The turbulent sea and the journey had taken its toll on this, sometimes, fragile young woman. Her husband, my dad, who's now, as we make our way to Christ Hospital taking his last breaths, was keeping watch. His boxer hands were patting her head with a damp cloth, murmuring words of comfort, scooting us, my brothers and me out into the hall.

"Go to the show," he commanded. And continued in a whisper so unlike him, "Your mother needs quiet."

A precocious, adventurous girl with her brothers, united in a mission, and with no further urging or commanding, make their way to visit this thing called a 'show.' We weren't sure what it was or how it would keep us quiet, but if dad said it, it would be done.

The usher, the one standing just inside the room where the 'show,' the movie was playing, stopped our entry and between gestures of tightened lips and furrowed brows, I guessed this was not a good place to find something to do. I suppose everyone plans, or at least, almost everyone plans these things, these shows, ahead of time; everyone who's not scurried off so that their moms can rest and have quiet.

We don't speak English, besides hello, goodbye; nor do we speak Greek. But the usher, who I imagined must have guessed we needed to find something to do that required quiet. I didn't beg. None of us did. Casamentos, we'd been shown, at least those of Salvatore's line, my dad who was now taking his last breaths, don't beg. I looked to my brother, Sal, and said, "Tell him we'll be quiet."
And Joe, Pippo, his smaller hand still in mine, restless, began his soft whimper like a newborn kitten's purr as it seeks his mother's warm underbelly.

The usher's face lightened, softened, his eyes gentled. He took my hand, the one not holding Joe's, put his fingers to his lips, that universal sign that sometimes irritated the gabby girl who always had something to say, and took us in. The room had seats, the kind that fold when not in use, on either side of the aisle down the center, connected to the other seats. We walked down that aisle to the front and the usher again put his finger to his lips and left after seeing to it that we were seated and quiet. And so it is that sometimes the unplanned happens.

Sometimes, I prefer it that way. Where a kind usher, an understanding clerk, find a moment's tenderness that affects a life, a lifetime and it is good.

Chapter 8
Steps

"There was never yet an uninteresting life. Such a thing is an impossibility. Inside of the dullest exterior there is a drama, a comedy, and a tragedy."
- Mark Twain

A lifetime of endless steps, hoping to get to the hospital before that last breath, like the last breath I remember taking before, going under water unexpectedly, at a crowded pool at Palisades Park.

It was July 1964. The Beatles invaded America as we had done previously. "The Leader of the Pack," plays loudly in the distance.

My niece, Joyce, an endearing nineteen year old, whose fastback Mustang reminded me of the waters that flowed at night in Marina di Patti has taken us to this theme park. Her car was blue, that blue that helped me re-visit the island left behind a year or so earlier. Where dad, who is taking his last breaths, while the roaches and mice, probably lulled by the hissing of the oxygen as its pumped into his failing lungs, scurry in the dimly lit night corridors, begins his journey.

But it is the blue of that fastback that drew me back, pulled me like the endless rhythm of the sea. The same sea, the same ocean, that I remember, when not visiting it in the car, the only car used for taxing the Sorrentini villagers to Patti, in the distance far below the plateau that holds fond memories of music and dance, and mom and dad.

After the August grape harvest, the grapes mashed and churned by men and women and, sometimes, children with bare, clean feet, the feat begins. The Guisa Vecchia plateau was where most, if not all, the villagers gathered; musicians, pasta, fresh sausage, and lots and lots of wine to celebrate yet another year of grapes and wine. This was a time when dad would gather mom in his arms, his boxer hands holding her gently, firmly, lovingly, joyfully, and spin and twirl and laugh his belly laugh, the one that came infrequently, but lasted long after.

He laughed. She laughed. The music played and Marina di Patti lay beneath capturing, holding it all in time only to ebb again and again same time next season.

It was this blue that brought us, my niece, her friends(and she had many), and me to Palisades Park on a hot July day. A day filled with noise and smells and screaming children, jumping, diving, swimming, then jumping and diving some more. Afloat upon an inflatable raft, at ease, allowing this new experience to fill me, I had not prepared, planned to take a full deep breath as I found myself, mouth open, terrified beneath the raft, under the pool's water. Hands grabbing, muffled screams from above, a deep breath, words, women, young girls, especially girls of eight should never say. I said them. Panicked, frightened beyond what frightened should be. There were no crowded pools with screaming, diving, jumping children in the village.

Take a breath. Take several breaths, my niece had said.

A breath. Many breaths. How many does my dad have left?

Christ Hospital, across from the pharmacy with its wide glass doors,that I never visited for a prescription. No, not this pharmacy across from which my dad was now taking his last breaths. Since we went to an apothecary run by a couple with tired faces and whose shelves were barren except for the occasional smattering of this glass bottle of aspirin or laxative and whose wooden planks creaked and moaned like I imagined the husband did each day of his life. More than a hint of gray framing his face, rather stocky and a stubborn, ill pallor to his face; a face that never showed any indication that he had been born with the natural inclination to smile. He would sometimes fill my dad's prescription of this or that. Deeply contrasting this somber man was his very tall thin wife whose smile came easily; welcoming me as a young girl. There was nothing exciting to welcome customers into this apothecary, albeit the squeaking sign that announced that this was a no frills medicine shop and that was all. Unlike the pharmacy across from Christ Hospital, with its colorful,seasonal motifs, and its ever-changing displays that enticed one to enter and make a purchase besides the usual prescription.

The clerk. A frenzied race to the elevator. Those interminable, deafening, "Dings!"

The footsteps, my mom's and mine, that seem to take us farther; the footsteps that lead us here so slowly; the footsteps that echo down the corridor to dad's room. Nothing and everything had changed at once. The hissing sound that I had heard just hours ago had been replaced by a sound that reminded me of those grapes smashed, ground, wet. Its juices sucked between bare toes. Each repeated stomp emitted yet another gurgle, a muted slosh like a child's rain boots slightly filled with rain. Slosh, gurgle, slosh, slosh. It was that sound that filled my ears not dad's laughter as he spun, and twirled, and whirled my mom with his dancer feet on the top of mountain, beneath Mt. Etna, on the plateau that overlooked the tranquil blue velvet waters of Marina di Patti.

Chapter 9
Apologies

"Truth does not blush"
- Quintus Septimus Tertullianus

Ushered into the dim lit, quiet hospital corridor, the doctor stood there, apparently distraught. Finally, the doctor looked to my mother, then to me and whispered those words, words of finality, solace, reality.
"I'm so sorry." The doctor whispered."He's gone."

Just like that, gone. The gurgling from within those sterile walls had ceased and it took my breath with it. I began to weep. My mom's only response was barely audible.

"Stop crying." She said."You'll wake others." Just those words. No hug. No gentle pat. No assurance of things being all right. I stopped my weeping and dried my eyes on my worn coat, the same white and black fake fur that had been bought at some second hand store or another, and that I cherished nonetheless. It stood out. Like innocent prey in an open field, waiting for the predator that lies in wait, camouflaged by foliage, waiting for just the right moment to end it all. It was the end and the beginning too. I stood by my mom, who did not weep. And so it went and I marveled at her composure and hated her simultaneously. My dad is gone and I must not cry. So I didn't. I didn't.

Our walk home was quiet and thick with the morning haze that had replaced the otherwise chaos and slow wandering to catch my father's last breaths. And our breaths, now, came slow. Their remnants were white puffs, like the wispy clouds of an old village sky in the middle of summer, reaching the air above our heads then just as quickly dissipating beyond. Each breath released for each step back home. Fatherless. Home, where my brothers were found awake and waiting. "Your father is dead." That was all that my mom said. Perhaps, it was all that needed to be said. No hugs. No gentle pats. It would have been, after all, out of the ordinary, when faced with death, to hug or say I love you; these did not exist in our house. Yet we felt the care that both of my parents had for each of their children. And I thought back to an earlier time, two years or so prior, when, Sal, was working, on weekends at my aunt, Katie and her husband, Joe's, fruit store on 67th Street on Bergenline Avenue in West New York. He never made it home one Sunday, as he had so many Sundays before. My dad, I remember, called my aunt and asked if Sal was running late that day. I remember my dad's face turn a shade I had never seen before, and as he put the receiver down, he turned to my mom and the quiet concern uttered in words I shall never forget; terror I shall always carry with me; my brother had not been all day and they, my aunt, Katie and her husband, Joe, as well as their son, Joe, Jr. had assumed he had left early without telling them. Frantic, my mom now in a frantic state of hysteria, her breath coming in gasps between sobs, clutched at her husband as he grabbed the receiver once again and called the police. They arrived shortly thereafter and questioned my dad, between glimpses of my mom, who now lay on the couch completely catatonic. "We'll follow up with West New York." One officer said. "And let you know as soon as we find out what is going on."

Dad paced as his boxer hands clutched one into the other over and over again while my mom, whimpered her eyes shut, repeating over and over again, Sal, Sal, Sal. It seemed like forever waiting helplessly each of us wrapped in a cloth of uncertainty, fear, and dread of the unknown. When the phone rang, dad quickly raced into action, punching the receiver off its base and slamming it against his ear. Sal had been found sleeping in the delivery truck's refrigerator. He was chilled, not having been prepared for what would come. He had been looking for a place to rest, feeling extremely tired after a full day of carting this and that. He found the perfect spot, or so he thought, on that very cold November day. Just like that, his eleven year old body had succumbed to the weight of working, lifting crates heavier than him, back and forth, back and forth, up into the truck and back again. He fell asleep. Minutes turned to hours and still he tried to remain asleep gathering crates of wine grapes around him for added warmth. He hadn't planned it this way. When he entered that truck in his thin sweater, the door shut. There was nothing in the truck but him, a crate of wine grapes, and the bitter cold for seven hours.

His arrival home, after dad and Grace, a family acquaintance went to bring him home, was filled with hugs and kisses. It was the only time I remember of hugs and kisses being shared by anyone.

Aunt Katie's and Uncle Joe's Fruit Store Front. 67th Street West New York, New Jersey 1966.

Here we were, though, three children huddled together sharing everything and nothing, because nothing was what we understood about death, our father's death.

Still my mom did not cry. She made her way to the kitchen and proceeded to make herself her morning coffee. We joined her at the kitchen table sitting in our assigned seats. Dad always sat at the head of the table; the seat by the window that faced south, the same direction that we had walked as our dad was taking his last breaths just hours

47

ago. We sat, my brothers and I, simply staring at the chair, my mom, then back to the chair. We looked toward the place that had harbored the garbage bag into which he spewed out yellow green phlegm each day, morning, noon, night and every minute in between. We noticed the bag had been where he had left it, a reminder of dad and his last breaths. We looked to the corner just to the left of where dad had sat, by the window that held a planter which dad filled with basil and parsley for his many culinary delights, but it was the corner that held our attention; its hooked latch on top hiding the contents of pickled eggplants, tomatoes, or squash. The same treats that delighted us, that were handed out sparingly as dad would have it.

Dad was gone. He was on a journey. We sat silently drinking our coffee with our mom and ate nothing. We watched, we listened, we waited. A lifetime of waiting. Dad had always prepared our meals. I began to think of things that would be changed.

"Dad, there's a bug or something in my tomato soup," I screeched one day over lunch.

My dad nonchalantly scooped it up and just as nonchalantly and commanding said, "Now eat, Anna." I did ignoring the idea that I was eating a bug infested soup.

"Let me see that," he yelled.

"You can eat it now," was all he said.

Dad believed in wasting nothing. And, if by chance, I didn't like the lunch he had prepared or the dinner, and decided I'd had my fill, dad would carefully wrap those leftovers and present them again and again until they were gone.

I didn't care for vegetables or deer meat or polenta, or myriad of other foods that kids hated but were good for you. You never tried things to see if you liked them; with dad, you just ate them. Quite simply, ate it, like it or not.

Dad however, was an excellent cook who would make his stuffed Italian eggplant with its seasoning of salt and a hint of black pepper, slices of garlic, and chunks of Romano cheese. I remember he would hold those slender eggplant slices off three or four slivers of peel, insert the knife into each of those sections and carefully stuff them with his magic, then fry them before immersing then in tomato sauce until they were cooked through. On good nights, when dad had gotten a special deal on the eggplants, we each had two; but on especially excellent nights, we'd have three. Then we'd have leftovers the next day.

On occasion, when the meat vendor would yell out his arrival across the street from our house, dad would go out and buy kidneys (they were legal to sell then), and cook them up with onions and potatoes and slowly simmer them with sauce for hours. That, unlike the liver, he sometimes tendered, I loved. Mussels, yet another of dad's specialty were meticulously scrubbed of excess barnacles and weed, boiled, cleaned again, then placed on a sheet, smothered with sauce and covered with cheese and baked.

Who would make the capozzella? The one that dad would bake till fork tender; those nights were my favorite. I remember vying with my brother Sal for more mussels, which dad would literally sell to us. Since my brother worked the pizzeria and was allowed to keep a dollar or two per week and I was given the same privilege, we would bite at the auction, which, more often than not, my brother would win; a nickel a piece. My younger brother, Pippo, who, always made mealtime a challenge of wills, could often be found being cajoled, bribed, and sitting on my mother's lap while she tried desperately to get him to eat something, anything. For years, dad had tried to force him to eat on his own, but mom always won, taking him on her lap and spoon or fork feeding him with words of comfort and a constant stream of pleadings; although they never worked,the efforts never ceased.

Snails (escargot to make them more palatable), would find their way to our dinner table whenever the street vendor advertised their availability. Dad would run down and return with a bag in hand. Then, he would empty the contents into the kitchen sink that had been filled with water. He tossed them around at first waiting for the thin layer of film to come away from the creatures. Once this had been somewhat accomplished (since some refused to be enticed), he would place them in a pot semi-filled with more water. It was an interesting sight when, in the morning, he would lift the cover and there they were, most of them, clinging to the lid, as if somehow, that would secure their fate. It didn't. He pried them from the lid and watched them fall back into the water. Emptying the pot, snails and all into the sink, he proceeded to pull them out of their shells and rub them with his salted boxer hands, then rinse and return them to their homes.

Once this had been done, he would drown them in a bubbling pot of his famous tomato sauce. Slowly simmering them till they writhed no longer and gather a scoop full or two and placed them on our plates. Not caring for these delights as much as my dad, my mom, and my older brother, I wrinkled my nose, held my breath and sucked out the contents of that shell into my mouth and in one gulp sucked down my throat along with enough bread saturated with plenty of sauce to stave off the rubbery texture of this supposed delight.

Those nights always reminded me of the days, after a rain, when Sal and I would go snail hunting in the mountains. Finding them rather easily, our buckets soon became full and we proudly presented them to our dad, when he was back in Sicily, or my mom, if he was not. Curiously, I decided to secretly recover one. What do snails do when left to crawl about, unencumbered by their inevitable fates. I placed it on the retaining wall that lead to the mountains from which it had been gathered, and watched it crawl leaving a path of ooze in its wake; holding it down in place, I noticed it writhe and spewed out a bubbly film of its own making. It reminded me of saliva; the longer I held it there, the more saliva accumulated. I'd had my fill of this observational fun and gently grabbed it up and released it down the grassy area just below and beyond the wall. At least I saved one, I thought.

A friend had generously given my father what he considered a true feast. It was Christmas time, and this particular friend had enlightened us about his family's tradition, one from upper Italy, that included eel at the dinner table. So it went one evening when he brought three live eels to our house. He outlined the preparatory rituals of skinning and cooking the writhing snake, as I saw it, and joined my dad in placing it into the pot of water, placing the cover over the pot and then weighing that cover down to keep the eels in check. The next morning, when dad went to release the slithering black eels from their container, he was faced with a quandary. The eels were gone.

"What the hell is going on here? Who took them out? Anna, was it you?"

I was known to have been a handful and dad rarely let my antics go unnoticed or unpunished. Not this time dad. Those things scared the dickens out of me. Perhaps, it was because they reminded me of those snakes that often writhed from the underbrush, slithered across our path, sometimes over our feet, as we, my brother and I, made our way up the mountain path to bring food to our workers in the orchards or fields. Snakes? I was glad they were gone. Dad wasn't.

"No, Dad," I told him. "I didn't take the snakes!"

A gentle knock was heard behind the washing machine next to the sink which had harbored the eels in their laden pot the night earlier. Dad inched the machine slowly forward, and lo and behold, there they were, huddled together, intermingled, entwined, as if they truly believed there was safety in numbers. Not today. Dad grabbed a dishcloth and carefully, though I think it was more apprehensively, he grabbed the eels one at a time and flung them into the sink. He grabbed the first, placed it on a cutting board, and chopped its head off. One at a time, he followed suit with the other two; the theory of safety in numbers was disproven that day.

He made slits lengthwise down the body of each, and then methodically began peeling away the dark skin letting it drop into the sink like thin wallpaper that had seen better days. A transparent coating of film, slime, and blood fell away with each peel. Cut into chunks, he prepared a white wine sauce with more garlic than I'd ever seen him use before, lots and lots of parsley, and plenty of wine to smother those chunks sizzling in the pot.

We looked at those chunks now in our plates and then looked at each other. It was the very first time I'd ever seen my father not force us to eat food we didn't want. Come to think of it, I don't think he ate it either save for the fresh bread dunked in the juices that were left behind after the eels had been fished out and dumped. I guess dad had limits to his tastes as well, free or not.

It wasn't so on an unusually chilly night back in Sicily. I must have been about six then and dad had just been out on the hilltops collecting mushrooms as part of the evening meal. My Nonna had always said that mushrooms were poisonous and would kill you.

"I know what's poisonous and these are good mushrooms!" My dad bellowed. I cried and I hid. I didn't want to die.

"Nonna said they're poisonous and I'm not having any!" No love lost between my Nonna and my dad.

"That old woman knows nothing about mushrooms. You'll eat them or you'll go to bed."

I opted for bed.

Nonna, perhaps sensing the night's events, made her way to my room, my head turned, blankly staring at the wall, my stomach churning and making gurgling noises. From under her apron, which she always wore even when not cooking in front of her brick oven that seemed to take up an entire wall of her house, she pulled out a chunk of her freshly made bread with a piece of goat cheese; the same goat cheese that she had churned and cured from her only goat.

"She's not to eat, old woman!" dad screamed.

Nonna watched me take bite after bite, then just as she had come in on her cat's paws, turned and made her way out the door. I smiled at nonna, imagined my dad's face at the turn of events, and ate the bread nonetheless. It was a feast and probably the best meal for someone who had come so close to death could have wished for.

Pasta was a staple in our home. It was always homemade pasta and mom made the best. There were days, rare as they were, when meat found its way into our home. It was usually pork but more often than not it was chicken. Mom had stretched out the neck of many chickens precipitating their death before she chopped off their head. Then she de-feathered and gutted them before cutting them into whichever shape was needed for that night's meal.

Pork, on the other hand, was a village party of sorts. Outside the butcher's shop sat a den that held the prey for slaying. On pig slaying days, more often than not, the villagers would gather and the butcher would make sport of the event. He would tightly knot a heavy rope around the pig's neck, anchor it to the post outside the den, then prompt any villager, who wished to partake in the slaughter, to simply get in line. The butcher would hand them the ten or twelve inch wooden handled knife and set the man, for it was always a man, to the task of goring the pig. The pig would fight the attack by shimming this way or that trying desperately, with his ear-piercing squeals to escape impales from those calloused hands brandishing the knife, to no avail. The village men, however, had a great incentive for attempting to put the pig down in one thrust. Anyone who could put the animal down in one gouge would receive some free pork.

I imagined what my dad would have done, since I don't remember him ever being present during one of these events. I suppose, he might have brought one of his guns. I don't believe there was anything in the rules about this method. Guns, for which dad was known to own, would surely have ended the pig without such suffering and sport. Dad could have used a gun. I never knew what a gun looked like; I'd only heard about it through conversations behind closed doors and thin walls. I didn't understand why anyone needed a gun, let alone four.

I found out the hard and troubling way that guns were serious. We were selling the contents of our home in Sicily prior to our move to America. A villager had come to purchase our armoire. Wishing to be helpful, I started to empty its contents. Reaching up on tippy toes, I felt a cold, odd shaped object in my hands and grabbed onto it. I then pointed it at the man who was admiring that piece of furniture. His face ashen, he took a step back, frozen. My dad quickly grabbed my arm twisted it sideways and relinquished the gun from my grasp. He made his profound apologies to the man and slapped me hard pushing me into the kitchen. I, the seven year old handful, peered in and saw my dad retrieve another three guns from hiding places and lay them out on the bed for the man who, I assumed, was highly interested in buying one. So went my introduction to guns though, at that point, I really didn't grasp the concept of their need or use. Still, dad owned guns. How many more were hidden and why was holding one such a big deal?

Yes, I supposed dad would use a gun since they were a weapon that would surely bring a pig down. Still, dad was not there as each man took turns with the pig until it resisted no longer, its blood oozing in rivulets down and in between the ill-cemented and aged cobblestone. Any life left in the pig was soon ended with a deep slice to its throat; unstrung from its earlier confines, the butcher with help from his workers, would then carry the carcass into his shop as the villagers headed home. The image of that pig, its body riddled with stabs to almost every inch of it, with its tongue lying askew to one side, its eyes staring into blank space, was an image of death. On a good day, as if any day is a good day when it is your last, the pig was mercifully held down by several villagers and without the sport of a slow death, had its throat slit. On those days, its blood would be collected in a bucket held in place to catch the flow; no announcements were made for that event; we knew a pig had been slain because there was pork for dinner, several dinners.

The animals in America, however, were store bought or sold by street criers and, on occasion, dad bought a goat's head which really didn't yield as much meat as the pork or chicken, besides the tongue and few meager scrapings of meat along the jawbone; it was a feast of sorts and a source of contention as well. It went something like this.

The capozzella's eyeball and brain were yet another material for auction. Usually, the child who got the eyeball the last time would not get it the next time. But, since we often forgot who had gotten it last, rarity being the culprit, we bid for that too. It wasn't so much that I liked the eyeball as much as I liked the feeling of victory. The goat's brain had a unique taste somewhere between a soft banana and overcooked pasta. It reminded me of ice cream. Ice cream that seldom found its way to our freezer, except for the occasional ice cream sandwich, which dad liked as well, and if they were on super special pricing. Ice cream from Mr. Softee trucks, that announced their arrival on each and every corner of Jersey City and most especially at the park where children gathered in droves on hot days. It must have been a moment of weakness when dad broke down and succumbed to our pleading; he bought one soft vanilla cone for us, my two brothers and I stood in a circle and took turns licking the soft swirls; one lick, pass it on until it was all gone. We knew better than complain about this arrangement and certainly did not complain if we noticed a longer, lingering lick of it. That was the only Mr. Softee my brothers or I ever had. In retrospect, I suppose, Sal and I could have spent our earned money on a cone, but rather, Sal chose to use some of his earnings on Love Comics and I preferred paper cut-out, or paper punch-out dolls; that is, until I discovered music.

It was 1967 and dad would, as always, give us money for our work. "Dad, can I have an advance for a phonograph?" I asked him. "I saw one at Cheap Sam's on Central Avenue. You won't have to give me any money until I pay you back. Can I? It costs $29.95 and I have ten dollars saved."

I got the money needed plus an extra 50 cents for a record. I scanned the shelves just behind the register. I scanned back and forth, back and forth. Unable to decide amongst the selections, I'd heard them before when I was sitting in the back seat of that Marina di Patti blue Mustang. Songs like,"To Sir With Love" by Lulu; "The Letter" by the Box Tops; "Windy" by The Association; "I'm a Believer" by the Monkees; "Happy Together" by the Turtles; "Kind of a Drag" by the Buckinghams.

Back and forth again and again and I could tell the salesman was getting annoyed because he kept releasing heavy breathed sighs. "Well, what do you want?" He finally asked me."Have you made up your mind yet? Come on, now."

There it was. "Hello, Goodbye" by the Beatles. It was the only record I owned for a very long time and I played it endlessly. So much so that I didn't care that I never saw a nickel for several months and beyond. Luckily, the phonograph had a radio as well; "Hello, Goodbye" was starting to skip too often, especially on Good-bye.

And so it went.

What now?

Who will make the wine? Or turn the soil in our laughable excuse for a garden behind our house; plant seeds of tomatoes, eggplants, peppers, cucumbers and tend to them each and every day from a worn out garden chair where he sat hose in hand and allow the trickling water to make its way down the rivulets he had created. Who would do that now? Dad was gone. "I'm so sorry," the doctor had said. Mom didn't cry.

I suppose it must have been late morning or early afternoon, not that it really matters, but my half-brother, the one who had admonished us about our talking to anyone, came meandering up our two flights of stairs. We stood by our mom, who upon opening the door for him, collapsed into his arms, her black dress crushed up against him, weeping, inconsolably so that I stepped back and wandered, questioned silently within my confused state. I could not cry in the hours of the morning after my father had taken his final breath, and my mom had not cried at all. Why would she cry now?

I thought back to 1966 when my mom had come home for lunch from the factory where she worked around the corner on Palisade Avenue. It was her latest changeover; mom seemed to change jobs quite often in those days. Some, she said, the money was not enough and she could do better since she had now become better at the craft, one that she had never been exposed to back in Sicily; some, she said, the overseers were horribly hot-tempered; and still others, her co-workers were evil and gossiping all the time. So she sat, the mail she had taken from the downstairs lock box, patiently awaiting her attention. Again, I wanted to be helpful and give her some down time, so I offered to read the one from Sicily.

"No, it can wait until I finish my lunch," she had admonished.

"Mom I can read Italian." I said."I'll do it for you."

"No."

"It's from your brother in Sicily."

An odd addressee, her brother, Giuseppe who had spent most of his adult life in Argentina; a letter I wanted to read for my tired mother. And so, I began reading. I remember it began with the perfunctory openings that most letters of little imagination and sincerity hold, "Hope all is well, etc." Then as I continued reading, stumbling over words that were illegible or difficult to recognize, there it was.

"I'm sorry to inform you that our mother is dead," I read.

My mother's fork dropped from her hands and her face became ashen as she looked at me with that look that says both, I hate you and I don't believe you. She tore the paper from my hands and re-read it. Her eyes filled and with one short gasp for air, she found her words and commanded me to go to the factory and tell her boss that she would not be back for the afternoon, her mother had died. I sat for what I know as only seconds and it hit me, overwhelmed me with disbelief and sadness; my Nonna, the Nonna who had saved me from death with her bread and goat cheese; the Nonna whose hand-sewn skirts, one blue, one green, each embroidered with delicate flowers and leaves along the hemline and suspenders; the skirts I had to give away because American girls don't wear such clothing that announce they are immigrants. My Nonna was dead and I had broken the news to my mom.

When I came back from the factory, my mom had already changed into a black dress. She was reading and re-reading the words with which I had just minutes ago impaled her, like the pig in Italy, not so long ago. Now, it was my mom who sat bleeding from her eyes, which were fixed on something I could not see. She must have hated me then, no more, though, than I hated myself.

My dad is dead and I hated her then. Thinking it was pretense; a widow needs to show some grief. Why not earlier? Why Now? And so I stepped back and watched as he consoled her with, "I know, I know, it's okay," he said. She seemed to understand those words of consolation, they seem to be universal; and mom had yet to acquire the full meaning of her new language, English, the language I had now mastered, the same language that I was called upon to use to interpret when mom couldn't feel the words.

"You're daughter talks too much in class," my fourth grade teacher, Mrs. Shapiro had said to my mother on conference night. I had accompanied her then and translated each and every syllable of what was said.

"Just smack her," I said. That was my mother's reply. Now it was mine. Just like that, "Smack her when she talks!"

I didn't hate her then, I was the translator and I feared that a lie would give me away. I believed my mom had this uncanny sense of understanding me even when I didn't understand myself. She'd know, somehow, she'd know.

But now, clinging onto my half-brother as if her legs would buckle under her, that forgiving nature, the part of me that tried so hard to understand possibilities and rationalize them in my twelve year old brain, guessed that she did not want to burden her children, she had to be strong for her children's sake. Thus, she had not allowed herself to cry. And, I suppose, if I continued to cry, had she not commanded me to stop, she might have lost control and her children would not know what to say or what to do for her. So she did not cry for them.

And so it went. My big half-brother left just as quickly and unexpectedly as he had come. Consoling. Holding. Comforting. Glancing past my brothers and me.

In Sicily, when someone passed they were placed on a makeshift altar in their home, candles holding vigil; one on each corner of the altar; one day, one solitary day. On the second day, some of the village men, those relegated for such services, would place the clothed and blanketed body in a casket, often made of simple pine, and carry it down and through the village peaks and vales to its final destination; Sorretini's only cemetery past the churches both old and new, up a steep hill and beyond the winding path that had a familiarity that echoed of final journeys.

Once the casket arrived at the gate, which to my recollection was never closed, the men carefully maneuvered it into a room. It was a solitary room with a makeshift floor revealing years of wear and tear and final journeys. It was here that the casket was set down and reopened revealing quiet and nothing more. And it was on one of those final journeys that I snuck into the room, squeezing my way passed the mourners, huddled close enough to feel one another's heartbeats, my mom included, reached that casket that held the quiet of my embroidery teacher, knelt quickly down before anyone could believe what I was doing or why, aghast and shocked, they watched as I kissed her drying face. A frenzy of calloused hands snatched me up and flung me toward my mother who quickly pushed me out of the room. In the serenity of the night and under the stars, I suffered retributions for that solitary act. I was scorned and even feared. Superstitions, and beliefs of possessions ran rampant; I would indeed, one day, fall prey to the latter. One does not kiss the dead. I kissed that gentle woman each and every time she tutored my lessons and listened to my ramblings and mothered me; I would kiss her now when I needed it most.

I managed a glimpse through women's skirts and men's orchard trousers; I watched as they unrolled a sheet of metal, inching it along the casket welding it at its sides, sealing, sealing; finality. I cried and cried some more. I was not consoled nor would I be. Some wore black, those distant relations she seldom spoke to me about; those she had no wish to see and, I know her wishes were followed.

Mom wears black and the upper sleeves of our clothes, my brothers and I, will be adorned with this band to allow the world to acknowledge our loss. We are in mourning. Our father is gone and services, arrangements must be made today. We are in mourning and when this period is over, our bands and mom's black dress will be no more. The arbitrary rules set forth by generations of the church, the clergy, ancestors; wear black and so it goes. One, two years for husbands, wives, mothers, fathers, children; months for other relatives; and so, I suppose, as your heart lightens so should the color of your dress.

Here we are following traditions, but the traditional four candles don't exist here. Dad is somewhere that is not here, home, the village pallbearers are long ago left behind with their sheets of metal and welding irons, their shovels and the customary bouquet of geraniums;

geraniums looked upon by the villagers of Sicily and my mom and my siblings and I, as we have been told, are the flower that are only used to pay tribute to the dead. Geraniums; for years I had feared this flower yet loved it just the same; so the arbitrary traditions set forth and beyond that I accept and question simultaneously. They smell pungent; they emit a certain milky substance from their stem when cut; but I realize, now more than ever, that geraniums can be found and gathered in the meadows and vales of Sorrentini all year long.

Chapter 10

Service

*"There is no greater sorrow than to recall happiness
in times of misery."*
- Dante Alighieri

My mom and her translator are were looking into services, as my aunt, the one from the pizzeria, had advised her to do. We had been informed that my dad's body had to be autopsied, whatever that meant, and , then it would be released to the funeral home. They needed to know which funeral home, or parlor as it was called back then, would be responsible for him after they were finished with the autopsy.

Burke's Funeral Home was located on Palisade Avenue across the street from the park, where dad had bought my brothers and me the one and only Mr. Softee ice cream cone. It was here that the mortician, the owner, John L. Burke, greeted us. A burly man with a bulbous nose and whose head looked like it could have crushed his otherwise, small-framed body at any moment. Still, he was very welcoming and a genuine half-smile crossed his face toward my mother as he took her hand in his and gave it a gentle squeeze. With me, on the other hand, he had apparently lost his, I suppose customary, familiar greeting for the bereaved, and didn't quite know how to greet me. So, he just smiled. Not a half-smile, but rather one that adults often show children when words fail them and confusion overrides habit. He looked to my mom and then glanced toward me. He suggested I sit in the chair in the hallway that led to his office and I explained that I am my mother's interpreter and will be with her every step of the way. I'm not sure if he scowled, frowned, or simply lost the elasticity in his face muscles; he simply nodded and led us into a room that harbored a desk whose sheen, a deep rich luster showing not even a hint of dust, much like our dust free home which, mom, insisted we, she and I, dust, sweep, wash, and scrub every nook and cranny each and every Saturday after she commanded my dad and brothers to leave.

Mr. Burke's desk announced that this overstuffed, oversized monstrosity, engulfed in gaudiness, was his and two chairs, almost touching, facing the desk and chair where he had now made his way and sat with his somewhat short plum fingers too small for his otherwise large hands, gathered together and began a slow, gentle utter of, what appeared to me, were scripted for just such service preparation. He would stop mid-sentence, wait for me to translate what he had said, wait again for just a bit for some sign from my mom, I suppose, then continue with the next fragment of a sentence.

And so it went for what seemed like forever if forever exists. He'd shuffle papers between glances toward my mom then back to me. I expected he'd hoped that my mom would suddenly understand and that somehow he wouldn't have to address me who then had to address my mom. I am sure that never before had he discussed funeral preparations with a twelve year old girl. Still he continued and I, subsequently, would turn to my mom and translate each detail. Would there be a funeral mass? No. Would you like a priest or pastor to come to the service then to the cemetery to say prayer? Yes. How many limousines would be needed?

I didn't readily understand what a limousine looked like; the only cars I had known included: a Fiat four-seater that would often taxi at least eight to Patti as needed; my dad's cousin, Roy's, a light blue Valiant, that he would often generously offer to take us, or dad alone, here and there. The here and there once included a trip to my Uncle

Barney's bar, or farm in Long Branch. I remember the bar with its wooden counter behind which a relatively young man would dole out this concoction or that, usually beer or wine though, to its eager patrons. I remember sitting in one of the booths where Uncle Barney had the waitress serve us lunch and asked if we wished a beverage.

"Beer." My dad commanded.

I could tell the waitress was at a loss for words. Her mouth slightly agape, she didn't even think twice to counter my dad's request, made a hasty retreat only to return just as hastily with beer in tow. We had just taken a sip, when my Uncle, who had left momentarily to oversee some business or other, came and whispered into my dad's ear. Our beers, not my dad's or mom's, were taken away and replaced with, the beverage I had now recognized by its captivating fizz which I watched intently before starting a slow sip through this thing tube called a straw. Later that same day, after Uncle Barney had seen to it that his presence would be felt even if he did leave for times on end, we all packed back into Roy's car, all that is except dad who rode to Uncle Barney's farm.

I so loved the farm. Its smell,its open fields. The chicken coop which my brothers and I were free to explore. It reminded me of the first time, back in Sorrentini, when an older friend, Bianca, had asked me to accompany her to her family's chicken coop to check the chickens before letting them out. She demonstrated how this would be done; she inserted her pinky finger into the chicken's rear while explaining exactly why she was doing this. One by one she checked the chickens and when she was satisfied that they were clear, she would set them out to the open pen

"Before we let the chickens go out into the pen, we have to make sure that they're not ready to drop their eggs. If that happens in the pen outside, the eggs will get crushed and my parents will know I didn't do a good job. I need them to trust me," Bianca said. It was known throughout our small village even if one did not speak to Bianca. People assumed that because she had an eye that seemed off, crossed and irregular that that also made her stupid and flawed and that she would never be able to do even the simplest task like the one we were to do today.

So I followed suit and stuck my small pinky, after wetting it with my saliva as Bianca had done seconds ago, and proceeded with this task. I wasn't sure what I was feeling except uncomfortable. Bianca, contrary to what the villagers thought they knew about her, immediately sensed my discomfort and simply asked me to watch. I admired that quality about her and we often spent hours together exploring this hill or meadow and even hiked up the trails to the ancient convents that were now hollow, crumbling walls of hope, solitude, and faith.

The ancient ruins were set high above Sorrentini and it was here that the tranquility allowed my imagination to take hold and free me from the sometimes confusing, antiquated, and judgmental world of the villagers below. Yes, they judged those who, according to them, needed judgment based upon nothing more than their narrow minds. Down there, in the village, where little boys made sport and just as evil, children gathered to watch and ridicule.

Gianni Popo was never seen playing in the fields, never accompanied his mother, the whereabouts, or very existence of a father unknown but speculated and gossiped about in the openness of the square where the old gaping mouth of a mythical animal streamed a constant flow of fresh water and where women gathered slightly in front of it to wash their clothes in the community wash basin talking about this neighbor or that who was not present then silenced if she happened by. Where Gianni's mother was never seen scrubbing, slapping, gathering, scrubbing and slapping garments upon the marble ridged slats that ran the perimeter of the open basin.

It was, however, not unusual to catch glimpses of Gianni Popo and his mother. And, as children, we gathered to watch the sport. Gianni Poppo was stripped naked, crouched, a jug in his hands, and his mother alongside with her tightly woven rope, lashing his bare body. And when it landed, muted whimpers echoed and urged the watching crowd, children mostly, into a frenzied laughter. I watched, on, ashamed for him. I did not cheer but that made me, in my own mind, no less evil and guilty of deriving pleasure from other's pain. She continued to lash at him all the way the slight slope that lead from their home to the community fountain where he had to rise, bared bodied, to fill his jug. Once this was done, his mother pushed and shoved him as they retraced their steps back to their house up the slight incline slamming the door behind them. This was Gianni Popo's life and I watched and did and said nothing. I just watched.

63

Thoughts running freely, wondering questions, about the women who were often brought to the town church screeching in horror, their faces contorted, their hair matted, their arms stiff in the tight grasps of several men as they escorted her into the church for exorcism.

"She's from Montereale, a town just below Sorrentini. She's truly possessed. Her poor husband just didn't know what to do with her. Look at her. She's obviously with the devil." Some speculated.

I skirted myself from behind my mother vying for a closer glimpse of this possessed woman just as the men were dragging her screeching, taut body toward the entrance of the church. I continued to watch as this woman, one of many who had been brought forth from this town or another, her hair matted against her scalp, her face, her dress covered in soot, screaming, wrenching, contorting her body, trying to take hold of something, anything that would assist her escape. All to no avail.

"Get back, Anna or the devil will get you too," my mom admonished.

I did, and wondered why Gianni Popo's mother wasn't taken to the church for exorcism as well. Surely the screams that were sometimes heard loudly and clearly, incomprehensible brutal words spewed at Gianni Poppo, were enough to sanction an exorcism. It never happened. And upon her death, she went alone, save the pallbearers who laughed while making sport of her pine box that teetered upon their shoulders. Gianni Poppo was gathered away and never seen again.

Here, though, in Long Branch, the coop was massive and the clucking of those chickens filled the afternoon quiet as my brothers and I were set off by my Uncle, with dad's consent, to explore the meadows and wooded areas just beyond. I felt at home once again. It was the one and only time I felt free once again.

My brothers and I strode the meadow and I knew that my brother, Sal, was probably wrapped in thoughts of the village as well. I could tell by the gleam in his eyes that he had spotted something of interest. Nesting birds high above in the treetops. I'm sure he thought about Sorrentini and the places where birds nested, their eggs lying in wait. It was there, in the buildings, high above the ground, where without coincidence, a ladder would often be leaning up against the structure and curiosity always won out.

"Anna, you go up and check the nest in the cutout of that side. Tell me what's in there, then I'll take it from there," My brother would say.

Snakes, that's what he really wanted me to fish out. If there were snakes in there, I would yell down from the top of the ladder and I'd move down to the next.

"No snakes, Sal." I'd tell him."Want me to come down or check some other openings?"

"No, I got it. Come down."

I did as he waited impatiently for his turn. Surely enough up he'd go, grab an egg and climb back down with it. He had gotten his prize for the day. I'm not sure why this was such a sport. I so preferred the days of tree climbing; fig trees were easy for me with my five or six year old legs; cherry trees, on the other hand, were not as easily maneuverable. Sal would ascend the trees, gather cherries, one at a time and in one full scoop into his mouth were gone but for the pits that he teasingly would often spit down to us.

"Not funny, Sal."I shouted. My younger brother, Pippo, and I wanted cherries. "Remember the nests, Sal? Stop playing or no more egg hunting," I threatened. It always seemed to go that way and eventually, Sal would send a rain of cherries to the ground for us. Marenas mostly, sweet, then bitter, then sweet again. And if the tree provided a bounty, we would gather as many as our hands would allow and bring them to my mom who would preserve them for the later months. No cherry trees. No fig trees. No ladders to climb. A Long Branch farm and memories.

Chapter 11

It Will Last

*"By protracting life, we do not deduct one jot
from the duration of death."*
- Lucretius

"Limousines? How many will be needed?" Mr. Burke urged.

I suppose he must have seen the befuddled look upon my face especially since no words came to me that my mom heard or understood him. He set about explaining what a limousine looked like and what a flower car looked like as well. I explained this to my mother and gave him my reply.

"One limousine. Two flower cars."

It continued like this for a while. Limousine. Fee. Pallbearers. Fee. Mass Cards. Fee. Plot for burial. Fee. Excavation of the plot. Fee. Headstone to be ordered. Fee. Preparation for viewing. Fee.

Newspaper announcements. Fee. With the ease of a salesman, savvy to the art of pickpocketing, convinced my mom to consider the need for a cement casing to protect the coffin. He assured her that this was a good investment because it would protect the coffin from the elements; saturating rains, vermin, and rot. She agreed; though admittedly, I never truly understood the need for such a casement. What difference would it make? Dad would never see it; nor would we. I suppose, in retrospect, it had more to do with mom's need to give the best and somehow, that casement and the supposed guarantee it gave of longevity, eased her aching heart. This was her husband who had taken her and their children to a great land of opportunity; it was the least she could do, especially since mausoleums, much like those in Italy, were unheard of, or at least, too expensive to consider. There would be no such homage as had been afforded my nonno and Nonna back in Sicily. And I reflected back and felt saddened. I remember, when nonno had been entombed in his, how I'd visit, place geraniums in the container held in place beneath it, and stare at the picture affixed to it. Dad would be placed in the ground. A place where, back in the village of the not so long ago, only those who were poor and could not afford mausoleums would be buried. Then, it came.

"Let me show you the caskets so that you can decide which you would prefer." Mr. Burke said.

My mind ran circles around itself. Unlike back home in Sicily, one didn't choose a coffin, it arrived, the body was placed into it and off they marched, the villagers, especially those closest to the deceased, followed the procession to the church, past the town square, up the winding hills and to the cemetery. It was that simple. In my mind, it was that simple. Pick out a coffin?

Coffin. Fee. The fee, however, is determined upon choice.

Mr. Burke rose from his chair behind the desk and ushered us into the hallway. I had not noticed the smell of decayed flowers and mustiness earlier, but suddenly, my senses had become greatly heightened. We passed a room with its open double doors that housed dozens of wooden folding chairs, and beyond those chairs, I noticed a wide open area before them. A crimson velvet drape hung solitarily along that opposite wall; it was a crimson that reminded me of death, blood, and finality. Crimson as if blood had been used to make it. Crimson so much like the blood that gushed and spurted from the slaughtered pig of long ago. Initially, I had overlooked the wooden structure, next to which two wooden sets of stairs lead entrance to nowhere, which rested just in front of that solitary drape, but there it was a reminder, of sorts, of Sicily and the laying out of the deceased. That much of death in America was similar; yet again, as I fixed my gaze still upon that wooden structure, death had become the same.

"This way," he said. "Just down the stairs. Let me turn some lights on and unlock the door."

We followed, my mom and me, the man with the bulbous nose and hands too large for his short fingers. My body tightened upon itself and my senses awakened to a smell of something unlike anything I had experienced before. Not so much of medicine like in a doctor's office, or even in the hospital when dad first began his journey, but rather like a chemical whose origin I did not care to know. It stung and filled my head with the thought of death imbedded within the walls of all funeral homes.

"Here we are." He said in a tone that could only belong to him.

We entered the room,Mr. Burke first followed my mom then me. A shudder of dread engulfed my being as I tried desperately to control my breathing. I would not let fear sink its fangs into my soul, but it did as Mr. Burke methodically and all too familiarly took us to each and every coffin that rested either on the floor, side by side, or up on slabs like tiers of wooden beds made for discomfort. Overwhelmed, I shuddered, my teeth clenched, I continued on with translation after translation as Mr. Burke recited the benefits and fees attached to each coffin he presented as he walked us around this all too small room that reeked of death and endings.

"This one is our top model," he said with a pride I had not known existed when death arrived. Models upon models. Bronze. Copper, Wood, and the choices went on as each and every breath I took caught somewhere between my lungs and throat. I translated.

"Surely, you might want to consider this one." He continued."It's not only quite beautiful but it has a silk lining and is meant to last for years on end. Look at the pillow. Here, feel how soft it is. It is our most expensive model but worth every penny and we certainly can talk about the price when we go back upstairs."

All translated. My mom quite simply shook her head, looked from coffin to coffin as if this was all natural to her, a look I envied. On a mission, she stood steadfast, never flinching, her breathing quite natural, her body relaxed. I, on the other hand, felt the room closing in on me with its walls covered with coffins; coffins that spoke volumes in my brain and all I could do was translate between deep wisps of breath, like a fog creeping eerily over a miasma of decay and waste.

"We'll take this one." My mom finally said. I translated, closing my eyes wishing all of it would end and that I was a wayward girl again chasing gypsies in their brightly colored caravans playing their tambourines and selling concoctions. I wanted to go home. Home, my home, Sicily where dad would visit now and then where I ran in fields and meadows, climbed ladders, sought out egg laden chickens, and waited for Sal to throw down cherries from those trees that I could not yet climb. Home.

Once he closed the lights and doors, we paraded back to his office where he shuffled his papers with pen in hand, began to itemize each and every fee, top of the line coffin included. Dad had a grand mahogany one with brass handles, which would be used to lift and carry him after the wake. I remember that word, 'wake'. Not from Sicily but from several years earlier when my dad's sister-in-law had died. She was his older brother, Joe's, wife. Since mom had refused to go, dad said I would go in her place. I did. I was eight and didn't fear what I did not know and sometimes what I did know, at least back in Sorrentini.

We entered a room, much like the one we would enter when my father was waked. Folding chairs made of wood, a drape against the wall that looked out at those chairs and now, the guests that occupied them. I remember, instant dread surrounded me as we approached the coffin, knelt, made the sign of the cross, and prayed. Though, admittedly, I truly don't remember praying but rather just looking upon this woman's face so unlike the woman, my mentor who had taught me how to embroider and spent hours just talking to me. No, my aunt, this woman, my dad's sister-in-law, lay, her face caked with an artifice, her lips sealed shut with a hint of pink seeping through. She lay motionless in her pink nightgown, a rosary carefully, purposefully, placed between her still fingers with their hue of artificiality about them. But it seemed to me, when I blinked, as I knelt there, she was letting go of her own wisps of air. I thought her chest was heaving, ever so slightly, negligible almost, but breathing nonetheless.

And so we sat, after kissing this one or that, hugging this one or that, we sat in two of those wooden chairs. I stared at the still woman in that coffin, her perfectly curled hair, her sealed eyes, her pale pink lips that almost matched her gown and she breathed. How can they bury someone who's breathing? I breathed, she breathed. I sat still and she lay still. This is a wake.

Never do I remember my mentor breathing. Never were her lips pink and fixed into a permanent smile. Her face wrinkled and drawn her hands haphazardly placed across her chest, she was placed in a pine box that was sealed with steel, welded and shut.

In Sicily, the women bathed, powdered, rubbed oil on to the skin of, and dressed in their finest dress or suit, the departed. Then with the help of the of village men, the women placed them on the fabricated altar used for just such occasions; candles strategically placed at each corner of the altar, prior to parading them up to their final home.

My aunt breathed, I breathed. Try as I might to look elsewhere, the faces that surrounded me, the walls that had seen more death than me, the bounty of flowers sculpted into crosses, hearts, sprays, baskets, I could not fix my gaze on those distractors. I returned my gaze to the lady in pink waiting for her final words. She's breathing; certainly, she can speak. She didn't. I didn't. Finally, I closed my eyes and remained in those memories of the not so long ago far, far from the here.

Thus, the decisions had all been made. We'll take this one. Papers shuffled some more. Fees and more fees. And as we exited, Mr. Burke made my mother an offer that made me cringe, and I hesitated the translation thinking of the possibility.

"If you need a place to live," he said, "I have an apartment upstairs that I will rent to you at a very reasonable price."

I translated and instantly noticed my mom's stature stiffen, her face however, never revealed the insult she had felt run through the course of her very being. She smiled and had me say thank you, but we're fine. All the way home I heard my mom repeat over and over, how truly insulted she was about the offer.

"Who does he think we are? Over the funeral home! "Those words over and over again. How could Mr. Burke know that we were a family whose pride ran deeply? Who never begged for anything they could not earn on their own, that my dad had bought a house, and that he once had more money than had probably ever gone through Mr. Burke's hands. My dad who, as I had been told, gave up his status as soldier in the gang, along with his money and property to save his brother, Barney's, life. So the story goes. Dad was a man, who held many jobs and had many escapades. I believed most of them after seeing bullet scars left behind when he wore t-shirts or went bare chested when he was preparing for a bath or the apartment got too hot for even him. Dad, whose escapades were sometimes retold during an evening meal or when mom and I were sewing the linings of collars, for women we

70

would never meet;dad, whose best friend and the one who had, in his younger years needed protection; dad, who set fires for a price, back in the day, managing never to hurt anyone in the process; dad, who was promised $10,000 from his son, Joe, for his last visit to Jamestown, New York; dad who worked and worked from the time he arrived in America, 1915;dad, who was an amateur boxer, owned a fruit truck; dad who bootlegged; dad who worked on the Eerie Lackawanna; dad who had to leave Jersey City and move to Chicago in the middle of the night with his then young family and his first wife, Anna;dad who seemed to command respect without uttering a word; dad who would give money to any and all who needed it.

No, we would not need the apartment over the funeral home, nor did we want it.

Chapter 12
Solace

"When you teach your son, you teach your son's son."
- The Talmud

Finally, we arrived back at the funeral home, greeted by Mr. Burke, who escorted us to the room that announced the beginning of the end and the end of a beginning simultaneously. Sal and I matched our mom's slow steps and inched our way forward to where my dad lay in front of that crimson drape and the stairs that lead to nowhere, up and around greeting that drape that held and witnessed the passing of many before. Slowly, we approached and peered into that coffin, the one that was the best; the one that would last forever in its casement that would stave off decay for a very long time. It gave me no comfort. Dad was dead.

My mom let out a whimper like a dog who been hit by a rock from this village child. She whimpered. Sal stood stone still. His face, that reminded me so much of my dad's and made me wonder how he must have looked in his childhood years, with piercing eyes and a small mouth, his mannerisms, overcome with the stillness of it all, just stared.

My dad was still; his hands, much like those of my aunt who had died five years earlier, and her husband, my dad's older brother, who had died two years earlier, were folded onto themselves, a set or rosary beads fixed in that lifeless grip. His face bore that unnatural hue, motionless, revealing nothing and everything. Still. I wanted to turn away toward the only chair that announced, welcome I am here to comfort you; come sit your grieving soul on my crushed floral pattern and arm rests that will give you support in your time of need. Come and sit a while. I would have, had it not been for my mom, who slowly turned and made her way to the chair before I did.

Visitors would be coming soon. The first viewing would be at 2:00 pm; this much we knew as my brother, Sal and I sat, each on opposite sides of my mother. Pippo, who had been terrified and screeched as he caught a glimpse of my dad and other sights that his eleven year old mind could not grasp, was quickly gathered by a relative and whisked away. So we sat, as one person after another made their way from the aisle just to my left, and knelt on the bench whose soft pillow matched the crimson drape. A sign of the cross, a few seconds or so of prayers, the same I had pretended to say at my aunt's wake, a pass toward my mom, a hug, a kiss, words sometimes stifled, rehearsed, sometimes loud as if announcing a great event, a turn toward my brother than me before moving on toward the aisle and back to a folding chair.

Faces. Many faces. Familiar faces, empathetic faces, knowing faces, comforting, compassionate. Don Miguelle and Donna Nunzia, who visited us often, spending hours talking of this and that with my mom and dad. I especially liked Don Miguelle who would often spend hours playing cards with me. When I wasn't playing cards with Don Miguelle, I would be playing cards with dad. Dad, who taught me poker and blackjack and who gave me money to play with and often I would win. He was so much older and better than me that even I knew the win was rigged. Dad knew that if he let me win, I would instantly take the money and run to the corner store to buy him his pack of Pall Mall. That was a game in itself; one I looked forward to, playing cards with my dad and winning even if it was orchestrated, though I'm still not sure he managed it.

And then I wondered,what now?

Immediately following Don Miguelle and Donna Nunzia were their children, Joe and Giovannina, and their son-in-law Umberto, whose house I had visited often. Giovannina and Umberto had a small child, a son, and I so loved playing with him and making him laugh. It was on one of those visits that I truly discovered how deeply Casamento pride and perhaps, arrogance ran. Wanting to be helpful to Giovannina, who was a relatively new mother, I offered to wash their dinner dishes, which I did. They, in turn, were so grateful they gave me a quarter. When I got home, I shared with my mom and dad what I had done while visiting them. Dad fixed his eyes on me and without releasing their telling gaze, bellowed, "Don't you ever think for an instant that a Casamento washes dishes for money. Ever." I never did.

Streams of people continued the ritual of entering, signing in, taking a mass card, kneeling, praying, hugging, kissing, mouthing words of comfort or solace and moving on. Judge Verga, who dad visited often at his office in Journal Square, the hub of Jersey City just south of the Stanley Theater,where dad spent many nights cleaning the remnants of the night's patrons. Yes, dad visited Judge Verga often. Following him was Mr. Maresca, a politician, who dad knew quite well for years prior to our arrival in America. And though it was never talked about, each and every holiday a gift basket would arrive at our home filled with the garnishments for a full holiday meal. What now?

The smell of tobacco and whiskey entered the room before he did. Paulie, MaryAnn's husband came in, went up to the coffin and just as quickly turned away. Approached my mom then was gone again. I noticed Grace, my mom's co-worker and the one who had driven my dad to West New York that day that Sal had been found, approach the coffin next. She lingered there awhile before making her approach to my mom. I noticed instantly my mom twist her face away to one side. For years after my brother had returned home, my mom had become suspicious of Grace. Mom insisted that Grace wanted her husband, my dad. Indeed, any woman who had any sort of contact with my dad, from the shop clerk to the pedestrian on the street, for some reason, my mom considered a rival. Not until later, did I understand the irrationality of her vehemence toward all women. Contrary, she wasn't irrational or delusional as I had thought in my innocence.

This continued over the course of three days. From 2:00 until 4:00 in the afternoon and beginning again at 7:00 until 9:00 in the evening. We sat. We greeted. Cordially, solemnly accepting condolences and those quick hugs or kisses and well-meaning or rehearsed words of comfort. We sat and while my mom, wrapped in deep thought of this time or one gone too quickly, I stared at the crimson drape then, my eyes magnetized to the coffin and my dad, I held fast to happier times. I watched him. His boxer hands still and I tried desperately to let go of the image of those still hands, once not so still, tying me to that chair or lashing out with his pant belt. I thought about the Hershey kisses that he loved so much; our trips to Jamestown; our visits to Fisk Park. Fisk Park located directly across from the funeral home where we sat for what seemed like eternity with the many faces coming and going; some sincere others obligatory. Yes, I thought of happier times; Fisk Park, which overlooked Hoboken beneath its wall and six foot metal fence, and where New York City lay before us with its grandness and its possibilities. It was Fisk Park on Palisade Avenue that dad would often spend some lazy summer days watching other men play bocce ball. Always on the same bench, watching for hours. His cane by his side, he sat. I remember mom sending me on a particularly hot July day to call him home for dinner. There he sat, and as I got closer, my back instantly felt the beginning twinges of anger, as my slow pace became an instant run. Some boys were tormenting my dad as he sat quietly watching unflinching at the assault of those miscreants. I picked up some rocks on my race toward dad and his bench, pelting as hard and precisely, as my arms would allow, trying desperately to fend them off.

"Leave my dad alone!" I shouted.

They didn't look back as they scampered off north.

"Anna, I have my cane." My dad said. "There was no need for rock throwing. I was just waiting for them to get closer. Let's go home." Just like that, we went home, dad with the cane he really didn't need and me with rocks still clutched tightly in my grip.

The second day, much like the first, flowed and ebbed with people. Still my dad lay in his silk covered coffin, the pillow plumbed and providing comfort, rest. Again I tried diverting my attention. I stared at the displays of flowers. First to the one my mom had ordered as it stood directly to the left angled to face the place where my dad's head lay. The pillow angled on the opposite side, the one ordered for my brothers and me in tribute to my dad. Dad hated flowers. Don't know why, he just did. Yet here they were. Not just a heart and pillow but many, many others as well. Flowers and more flowers, enough to fill two cars, that had been ordered, and then some. Carnations, roses, gardenia, baby's breath, and some I did not recognize. No geraniums.

All was quiet except for the occasional whimper of this visitor or the next while dad lay motionless in his coffin. We, my mom, my brother, Sal, and I, too, sat motionless. Mom had made it clear this would not be, as she had seen at my uncle Joe's, funeral a festival where everyone seemed to ignore the somberness of a passing, and chattered and even laughed as though they were attending a birthday party or wedding. No, mom would not have it. All fell into suit and paid their respects, then quietly took a seat somewhere behind us.

I watched my half-sisters, Josephine, and her husband, John sitting in the seats across the aisle. I had played badminton at their house once; rather poorly, but I played. My other half-sister, Marie and her husband Seymour, sat next to them. I so loved Marie and Seymour, and my sister, MaryAnn who made my first Christmas memorable.

All the kids in school had been talking about this fat old man with a red suit coming during the night and leaving presents of all sorts if you had been good during the year. We woke, my brothers and I that first Christmas to find nothing. And in my eight year old mind, I assumed I had been bad. I visited MaryAnn's house the next day, where there, under her white tree with its bright blue Christmas ornaments, was a neatly wrapped package with my name on it. It was a game of Chinese checkers. Shortly thereafter that same day, Marie and Seymour came by and presented me with again neatly packaged boxes. It was my first fashion doll, Tammy, complete with case and clothes.

It didn't end there with Marie and Seymour. Seymour, an Albanian, who for some reason dad deeply detested, would make a challenge of getting good grades. Each E, excellent in those days of the sixties, he would give me ten cents; a G, for good, would merit five cents. And most certainly, an F, failing, wasn't even a consideration. I maintained my E and G standing from third grade on. After a while, it wasn't even about the reward but, in my young mind, I was one of those weird kids who actually liked school and learning,my favorite subject being writing.

I looked to dad again and remembered his high expectations. He was always making sure that my homework was done to his satisfaction before I got a snack and then began working on colors. I remember his pride when I won second place in a district wide essay contest. Dad, who in his few words, could say a great deal. Like my father, Sal also said little but owned a stare that reminded me so much of my dad, commanded obedience, compliance, and acknowledgment.

My uncle Bernie, and my dad's cousin and best friend since forever,

Roy, sat behind us. Occasionally, I'd see Uncle Bernie's hand reach out and pat my mom's shoulder. And for some reason, not readily understood by me, I could sense her recoil at the gesture. Still, Uncle Bernie continued. At times, he would get up from his wooden chair and approach the coffin, stand and just stare. This, this brother, his brother had saved his life once upon a time.

The loud wail directly behind us, was ear piercing. Sob after sob and words of comfort echoed the otherwise quiet room. It was my half-brother, Bernie, who was crouched down next to his wife, Marianne's, chair. Initially, I thought the reality of my dad's passing had finally reached him, it was not so. I suspected, since he had not shed a tear until now, a few moments after his wife's arrival on that second day, that he was trying to win his otherwise I'm ready this time for sure to divorce you argument with his wife. She'd had enough, I suppose, of his parade of mistresses and oaths to make things right. She forgave him that much I knew. She had given in to this poor grieving man who had lost his pop.

Joe, my other half-brother, anchored next to his son, Little Joe and his wife, Betty, sat then rose paced, sat, then rose and paced some more. A caged animal. At one point, I noticed my three half-brothers in a corner whispering in an animated manner that emitted an anger and resentment of its own. It seemed to grow in magnitude as they looked toward where my dad lay on his soft pillow surrounded by flowers he hated. Joe was the half-brother who had promised my dad $10,000, which my mom had been advised of by my dad during his journey in the hospital. Tony was more animated than either Big Joe or Bernie. His face reddened with apparent anger as he grabbed hold of Big Joe's arm at one point, then, perhaps sensing the eyes upon them, let go and headed to a solitary seat, the last one in a row of others that were occupied.

Tony, who for some reason, dad never really respected. When Tony visited, he was if anything tolerated. I never understood why. Tony would visit with his wife and their four children; always with his wife and four children and never a mistress or their child, as Big Joe had done on numerous visits. I so loved Tony's visits, and while dad prepared meals, as he always did when his older children from Jamestown visited, a full spread unlike those meals he had prepared for my mom, my brothers, and me. They were meals that included the best cuts of meat, the best vegetables, cold cuts, vegetables that weren't bruised, this he did for them. We never questioned why this was so, it just was when they visited; those visits I liked not so much because my brothers were there, but rather because we tasted foods otherwise ignored.

I'd grown accustomed to those parades of putanas, as dad would call them, so when Tony came to visit, I fostered a respect not privy to the others; Tony, who brought his wife and children, three boys and one girl. Dan, his second son, would often bring his guitar on which he would spend hours playing or teaching me chords and on rare occasions, would even allow me to hold and strum its strings. I so loved those visits. Tony with his gentle nature and culinary masterpieces, the same culinary masterpieces that dad was so familiar with preparing. What caused this dissension? I never knew.

On the last day of the wake, somewhat accustomed to the stillness of it all, I was overwhelmed with wonder and appalled all in one. The stairs that rested at each side of the coffin and lead to nowhere, though in retrospect, I suppose they were too cumbersome to move and may have been used for cleaning the crimson drapes, those stairs, I discovered did lead to somewhere; my sister, MaryAnn's solace.

I watched as she approached the steps to the left of the coffin, the ones closer to where my dad's head rested, slowly as if her feet were encased in ballet slippers, she took one step at a time. The first step, then I saw it. She was holding a camera. She aimed and, I suppose, unsatisfied with the view, inched her feet, one at a time, ever so carefully, quietly on kitten's paws, as if any sound might wake, our sleeping dad, to the next step and aimed. Again, camera still in hand, she climbed the third, with two more to go, step, aimed her camera, re-aimed this way and that; a click, a flash, another click, another flash and descended those steps just as noiselessly as she had gone up. Approaching the coffin, she stood before it, just where his head lay still with its soft pillow and silk cloth, and watched. Her head tilted the same way as my dad's, she reached out her hand and gently touched his hands. She let them rest there while I watched her, unable to actually see the look of solace or grief or tears. I watched as she stood with her hand resting on my dad's.

And so on that final day, a final goodbye. We entered more quietly than I thought any human being was capable of being. We sat in our wooden chairs, my mom's crushed floral one that held her arms in comfort and stared. Just stared waiting and waiting for something that we hoped would come or never come; a collective breathing of family wrapped in memories, moments, minutes, hours, and years, far from the not so long ago of a small village that dad would never re-visit.

The pastor approached the casket, made the sign of the cross, and then faced the gathering. He spoke of passage, of God, the afterlife, grief, family, and prayer. Followed by Mr. Burke as the pastor made his retreat, who instructed all to pay their last respects, a final farewell, beginning with friends, followed by distant relatives, down the line to my mom and her young children. With the exception of Bernie, who remained behind, all followed the directive.

We watched as each approached the coffin, when I noticed that the kneeling bench had been removed, as had the flowers save for the heart and pillow. Our turn came too quickly. My mom approached, my brother, Sal, and I at each side of her. His face was as it had been the days previous; his still lips revealing all and nothing.

We watched mom behave unlike what I had experienced in the hospital where I was not allowed to cry, and unlike the crying she showed when Bernie had come immediately after dad died. She sobbed, clutching her arms against her chest. I cried. Sal cried. Bernie came up quietly behind her, took her in his arms, turned her toward him and helped her find her way to the door and the waiting limousine. Sal and I, alone, crying saying goodbye, turning and walking the steps mom and Bernie had just walked.

The limousine followed two cars full of flowers, the heart and pillow visible through the back window of the hearse that went before our limousine. Cars followed, headlights on. Down Palisade Avenue, a right onto another street, then a left onto Franklin Street, slowing in front of the house which harbored so many memories both good and bad; though, willingly, the bad relinquished their hold and with each breath I took, faded in the exhale of my being.

Steady rainfall replaced the slight drizzle on that cold November morning as we made our way to Hillside Cemetery in Lyndhurst, New Jersey, where dad's cement casement awaited. I watched the hearse with my dad and the flowers he did not like through the wet of the weeping skies and held my hands still upon my lap, an imaginary binding holding them in place now. My mom sat there in her black dress, one resembling the many she would wear for the next few months. She wore black until a relative convinced her to replace the black with colors; this is America. You're American now.

We wore our black bands over our outer clothing and only when my mom replaced her black for colors were we allowed to do the same. I wanted everyone to know I was grieving the loss of my dad who said I would go to college and who showed me how to play poker and blackjack, who trusted me to deliver his homemade wine, who nursed me back to health when I was sick, who took me to Jamestown with him on more than one occasion. The questions came when I went back to school about my band and I sensed puzzlement, and knew the whispers I heard were about that band. It was of little consequence. My dad was gone. He hadn't been breathing as my aunt had been when I went to her wake. Now that I was twelve years old, I realized that the breaths she was taking were really my own ebbs and flows of rhythm from deep within my chest. No, dad was not breathing.

But it was the weeping of that November morning that brought little comfort as we proceed up the hill and, the cars parked with its passengers waiting, waiting for finality to begin yet again. The coffin, my dad, had been removed and gathered up by pallbearers along with one other man precariously holding the remnants of those now crushed and empty spaces where flowers were left mangled in the place where the coffin had been. We walked up the muddy incline to the grave site whose perimeter had been covered with green heavy plastic the same plastic that creased and gave way to the muddy earth beneath. My mom, my brother, Sal, my half-brothers, their wives, my half-sisters, their husbands and a few relatives, stood near the pastor as he once again spoke to us. The sound of rain hitting the umbrellas the director had provided;umbrellas that were of little help as the rain had angled its flow and was hitting our legs and our hands, and found its way to our faces. The tears that were not shed willingly would be there nonetheless. The rain hit the flowers, some of which were pressed against the coffin while others were scattered haphazardly and without care. Just as well, I supposed; dad hated flowers.

Mr. Burke who had been standing next to the pastor now announced that the services were concluded and the limousines were waiting to return us to the funeral home. My half-brother, Big Joe, approached my mom and I translated his offer of dinner at a restaurant.

"No," my mother said.

"It's customary, Carmela." Big Joe said directly to her.

"Chi ti pari festa?" (What do you think this a party?) She protested. I had never seen my mom have a cause to be so stern, stubborn, commanding in her tone. I had so much to learn about this woman of whom I had witnessed the tirades and tantrums on many occasions. Her threatening my dad with a lamp that she held precariously close to his head, the menacing look upon her face revealing the seriousness of her threat. I knew of her stubbornness. Days upon days she went without speaking a word to my dad because of this argument or that. I remember the pull that each had upon me as each would, when the other wasn't around, share this tidbit or that about the other. It would end eventually, this much was certain. Usually, this end would come when a visitor came to our house forcing my parents to break their silence, their avoidance.

In Sicily, when someone died, it was customary, an unspoken rule, a tradition, one did not turn lights on at night and certainly not during the day. The stoves remained cold as relatives and neighbors upon neighbors brought food to your home each and every day for weeks. But this was America.

"Carmela," Big Joe urged."We'd just like to be together and remember our pop."

Again I translated and she acquiesced on one condition. It would not be a restaurant but rather back at our home on Franklin Street. Anyone who wished to join was welcome she had me repeat in English. Mom's offer was passed along and a decision had been made; they would come back to the house. My half-brothers, their wives, my half-sisters, their husbands and just two close friends, Don Miguele and Donna Nunzia. Once we got back to Franklin Street, with our entourage in tow, my mom began scurrying about grabbing this and that from the refrigerator and before we knew it the table was filled with all that my mom could think of on the spur of the moment. Of all things, mom cooked escarole with lots of garlic and tomato sauce, provolone cheese, salami, prosciutto, olives, and the pickled eggplant and zucchini dad had made that past summer. She scurried me off to the bakery where with great determination, I directed a look at the baker which said, I don't think so, bought fresh bread and hurried back home around the block.

I watched as my family and friends grabbed at this and that and seemed to savor the meal that dad might have served us but not his sometimes visiting older children. Still, here they were devouring every morsel and commenting on how fantastic it all was; the best meal they had in a while. And so it went until, the food had been spent, the conversation lulled and long rides home tolled by the ticking of the clock.

Mom busily cleaning even as the last of them, stay for Don Miquele and Donna Nunziata and Roy, each made their way to the door. Quick good-bye and hugs that seemed more obligatory than sincere, I closed the door and locked it behind them. Our friends remained and chatted about this event or that they recalled of my dad. Mom sitting listening. Listening.

When the mourning period was over, I went home and did what I had done for a few years; I had an affinity for this new language and tried, especially when I was hurt or sad, to write. That night, I reflected back to the events of the past few days. This poem contained feelings that remain with me still.

When I Die

When I die, I will not lament the golden road outstretched to its Own will

I will not pine the hunger for unsatisfied passion.

I will not hold in judgment those seeking only my survival when I yearned and sought to live instead.

I will not stand unwelcoming at the foot of the altar

All those before me who know not where I loved.

I will not yearn another second in the existence of that translucent Solitude.

Alone I will not go forth-back and up

Again.

I will not question the moment that will follow

All those that came before-

I will not hollow out my heart
Replace it with cotton clouds of doubt
This I will know-
That I will know-
And in the knowing will be my existence
Still.

XXXX

Epilogue

Within months, my mom had the house renovated. Walls were torn down. New ones replacing them; the kitchen modernized. All debts accrued by my dad, paid. Never had she received a penny or a phone call from her husband's grown children. She continued working her two jobs. My brother, Sal, worked his shifts at the pizzeria where I also worked on weekends. I sewed collars on weeknights and sometimes on weekends before going to the pizzeria at 3:00. The money she earned, she alone managed. She kept us in fine clothes, provided good food, and tried to supply us with the wants not just the needs. We didn't need to eat leftovers unless we chose to eat them. The fruit was never bruised and the steaks weren't just for company. I took over dad's responsibility of preparing evening meals. If it wasn't something I'd learned to prepare at the pizzeria, my mom would give me specific instructions on what to cook and how to cook it. So it was. I had become dad,but mom had found her strength; a strength I knew existed all along; a strength that was awaiting release; a strength that perhaps, may have arisen from need. Still she found it.

I no longer slept in the thoroughfare between bedrooms, bathroom, and kitchen. I shared my mom's bed. And even though I was a restless sleeper, much like my dad, walked often, screamed loudly, and whimpered softly, we shared the bed.

Uncle Bernie visited several times, until mom shared that his visits made her uncomfortable and she no longer took his calls. Thus, we never saw him again until his wake two years after my dad's. Roy still visited quite often and was always welcomed. Don Miguelle still played cards with me while his wife, Donna Nunzia, and my mom gossiped. I never saw MaryAnn after that or any of my other older half siblings.

I bought more vinyl records, watched American Bandstand on Saturday mornings and, not to my surprise at all, my mom would take a break from her Saturday chores, just as I was allowed to do during Bandstand, and dance. Just dance!

About the Author

Anna Casamento Arrigo was born in Sorrentini, Sicily and came to America with her family and settled in New Jersey.

After suffering a stroke, she turned to writing as a means of expressing her innermost thoughts through visionary prose. Inspired by music, poetry, and the classics of literature, Casamento Arrigo truly encompasses the breadth and scope of the written word.

Having taught inner-city students prior to her stroke, Casamento Arrigo understands full well what it means to need inspiration. Between the success found at her hands, and the successful impartation of love, creativity, and understanding, on to her five children and her seven grandchildren, Casamento Arrigo has accomplished a great deal.

She still lives in New Jersey with her husband, Vinny.

This is her first memoir.